She stood uprigh
into a fist with h
gripping the har
they hurt.

"Enough!" she said through gritted teeth. "Enough, enough, *enough*!"

Hunter spun around to face her just in time to see her toss her hat on the ground, yank off her wig, throw it down as hard as she could, stomp on it several times, then pick up her hat and plop it back onto her head.

Her breathing labored from the heat and her outburst, Skyler stared at Hunter while he stared back at her. They stood like that for several seconds, just staring at each other, before he asked, "Feel better?"

It took a moment for his question to register— it hadn't been the one she had prepared herself to answer. She breathed in deeply and then laughed as she exhaled. "Yes. Much."

Skyler knew that this wasn't the end of the discussion between them. But Hunter's willingness to keep focused on the job and ignore the fact that she had just pulled off a wig and stomped it into the ground was exactly what she needed.

"Good." Hunter turned back to his task. "Now let's get back to work."

Dear Reader!

Thank you for choosing *She Dreamed of a Cowboy*, the fourteenth Harlequin Special Edition book featuring the Brand family.

She Dreamed of a Cowboy is a humorous, heartwarming book that features the once-in-a-lifetime love story of Hunter Brand and Skyler Sinclair. Former reality TV star Hunter Brand has forsaken his public fame to focus on his family's expansive cattle spread, Sugar Creek Ranch, in Bozeman, Montana. Hunter is serious about his profession and his family's cattle legacy. He's a real cowboy doing real ranch work; and for the life of him, Hunter can't figure out *why* his father, Jock Brand, agreed to have a tourist stay at Sugar Creek Ranch for the summer during a pandemic.

Skyler Sinclair isn't just a cancer survivor—she's a *victor* who beat a rare form of lung cancer. In remission now, Skyler takes the trip of a lifetime—a dream come true—to a working cattle ranch in Montana. The fact that her childhood crush, Hunter Brand, from the TV show *Cowboy Up!* will be her summer ranch guide only makes the trip feel more surreal and special. But, as Skyler soon discovers, her childhood dream doesn't exactly match reality. Montana is beautiful but also hot and buggy; ranch work is exhausting and Hunter would like to ship her back to New York on the next available plane. Only Skyler knows something that Hunter doesn't—beating cancer has made her tough. No matter how much the cowboy wants to send her packing, Skyler isn't about to quit.

Falling in love with Skyler isn't a part of Hunter's plan— she's a city girl who doesn't seem to fit in with ranch life. But she is also quirky and sweet with an inner strength that is intriguing to Hunter. The way she sees the world—the way she sees *his* world—makes him begin to appreciate the simple beauty unfolding around him. Skyler is shocked to discover that the cowboy of her teenage dreams is actually interested in her, but the first moment their lips touch, Skyler knows that Hunter Brand is the man who is going to make all of her cowboy dreams come true.

This is one of my favorite Brand family stories and I hope you enjoy reading it as much as I enjoyed writing it.

Happy reading!

Joanna

She Dreamed of a Cowboy

JOANNA SIMS

HARLEQUIN

SPECIAL
EDITION

Recycling programs for this product may not exist in your area.

ISBN-13: 978-1-335-40474-9

She Dreamed of a Cowboy

Harlequin Enterprises ULC
22 Adelaide St. West, 40th Floor
Toronto, Ontario M5H 4E3, Canada
www.Harlequin.com

Printed in U.S.A.

Joanna Sims is proud to pen contemporary romance for Harlequin Special Edition. Joanna's series, The Brands of Montana, features hardworking characters with hometown values. You are cordially invited to join the Brands of Montana as they wrangle their own happily-ever-afters. And, as always, Joanna welcomes you to visit her at her website, joannasimsromance.com.

Visit the Author Profile page
at Harlequin.com for more titles.

Dedicated to my beloved father:

Even though you don't read my books
because of the naughty scenes,
every hero has a little bit of you in him.
I love you to pieces and I am so proud
to be your daughter.

Prologue

"Do you realize that I am on the verge of answering a very important question that has plagued womankind for centuries?" Customer-service representative Skyler Sinclair tugged on the golden blond wig she had donned. The hair was thick and straight and cascaded down to the middle of her back.

Skyler spun around to face her father, her heavy mane of blond hair swinging around her shoulders in the most satisfying way. "Do blondes *really* have more fun?"

Chester Sinclair was standing just inside the front door of her garage apartment, his arms crossed in front of his chest and his brooding dark eyes a match for the frown on his face.

"Why the wig?" her father asked. "You've never been ashamed of your hair or your scars."

"I'm not ashamed." Skyler turned back to her reflection to adjust the wig a bit more. "I'm just not about to show up in Bozeman, Montana, looking like Skyler the Cancer Patient."

"You *are* a cancer patient," her father reminded her.

"Correction. I *was* a cancer patient. Now I'm a cancer victor!" She punched the air like she was a boxer training for a fight. "I'm a cancer-crushing badass, that's what I am!"

In the middle of her tiny living room, Skyler planted her feet on the ground, hands on her hips, and lifted her chin like she was a superhero. After a second of holding the pose, she suddenly felt weak and dizzy, like her legs were going to buckle right out from underneath her. With a self-effacing laugh, Skyler folded herself into a nearby chair with a deep sigh. "Well, maybe not back to superhero status just yet."

As he had been from the second she was first diagnosed with a rare form of lung cancer, Chester was at her side.

"You *are* a cancer-crushing badass." Chester kneeled on one knee by the chair. "But you've got to be careful, Skyler. Don't overdo it. You're still so weak. Wait awhile, let all this virus stuff blow over and then go. It's not the right time."

"Time," Skyler said in a wistful voice as she tugged off the blond wig to expose her own patchy strawberry blond locks. "Time is a funny thing, Dad. I used to think I had all the time in the world. Now I know that I don't." She met her father's eyes. "None of us do. I always had an excuse why I didn't have time to do this or to do that. I was forever putting things off because—" she shrugged "—let's face it, I was too afraid to try." She patted his hand to reassure him. "I'm not afraid anymore, Dad. Cancer taught me the most valuable life lesson. All we have is right now. The time is *now*. Not tomorrow, not next week or next year. *Now*. I can't wait. I *won't* wait. I can't waste this second chance I've been given by beating this thing."

"Montana is too damn far away." Chester sat back on his heels with a grumble.

When the light-headedness subsided, Skyler pushed herself upright. "That was always one of my excuses for not going. Too far away, not enough money, not enough time. But you know that I've always dreamed of Montana." Skyler heard an emotional catch in her own voice. "Always. I've dreamed of the horses and the mountains and the wide-open spaces. Fresh air. I've dreamed of what it must be like to camp out under the stars with a herd of cattle grazing nearby…" Her voice trailed off a bit. "The smell of a campfire. I've dreamed of that life ever since I was a little girl. Don't you see? Montana isn't going to be just being some unfulfilled wish on my bucket list. It's going to be my dream come true."

Chapter One

"I'm here now, so let me go," Hunter Brand said to his father as he strode into the lobby of the Bozeman Yellowstone International Airport.

"Represent the family well, son," Jock Brand reiterated for what seemed like the one hundredth time. "Remember that, like it or not, you represent Sugar Creek Ranch."

Hunter hung up the phone, slipped it into his back pocket and then pulled the black bandanna he had tied around his neck up over his nose and mouth. How in the world had he managed to pull this summer detail? Babysitting a spoiled city girl who'd convinced her father to let her play cowgirl for a summer? Sugar Creek wasn't a vacation spot for bored socialites; it was a multimillion-dollar cattle operation. They did real work on the ranch and Hunter couldn't fathom why Jock had decided, seemingly out of the blue, to open the ranch to a tourist for the summer.

"Excuse me." Hunter smiled with his eyes at the pretty young woman at the information booth. "Did a private charter arrive from New York City?"

Hunter thought that he detected a hint of sympathy in the young woman's eyes when she pointed toward a baggage carousel where a slight woman with long blond hair was standing. The woman had a collection of suitcases, which looked like they were covered in vintage floral wallpaper, balanced precariously on a luggage cart. Her back to him, his tourist was staring up at a T. rex skull mounted at the center of the carousel.

"Thank you." Hunter tipped his hat to the young woman.

While he walked toward his summer ward, Hunter took in the expensive cowgirl hat, boots and dark denim designer jeans that hadn't seen a speck of dirt or work since their purchase. As he drew closer, the more irritated he became. The tourist looked like she could be snapped in half by a strong gust of wind. And then a thought popped into his brain. Maybe his summer wasn't ruined after all; this woman wouldn't be able to handle ranch work. Especially if he threw some of the tougher, dirtier, smellier jobs her way right off the bat—she wouldn't last one week, much less an entire summer. He'd have her racing back to her posh life in the city before the end of the week. Who could blame him if he gave her the experience she said that she wanted?

It was with that thought in his mind that Hunter greeted the tourist.

"Are you Skyler Sinclair?"

The woman gave a little start and then spun around with a laugh. It was a sweet, tinkling, joyous laugh that he immediately liked in spite of his intention to dislike everything about her.

"Yes." Skyler looked up at him, the corners of her eyes crinkling with a smile. "I am."

For a split second that seemed like slow motion, their eyes met and held. Skyler was wearing a mask, which drew his attention wholly to her large violet-blue eyes. Lovely, wide, expectant eyes that appeared to be completely without artifice. Then those eyes widened with a flash of recognition.

"Hunter Brand." Skyler said his name with a breathiness that stroked his ego in just the right way.

Hunter cringed inwardly. He had never met Skyler, but she seemed to know him. When he was a teenager, he had participated in a reality TV show, *Cowboy Up!*, and he'd never managed to live that down. After all these years, there were still fan clubs dedicated to him. God help him, he hoped Skyler wasn't a stalker.

Skyler must have read the question in his eyes because, filling in the silence between them, she explained, "I saw your picture on the Sugar Creek Ranch website."

Hunter wasn't sure if he believed that was the whole story, but it was good enough for now.

"This is amazing." Skyler pointed to the T. rex skull. "The nice woman at the information booth over there said that the Museum of the Rockies is open. Do you think I'll have time to go there?"

"I don't know," he hedged. "There's an awful lot of work that needs to get done at the ranch. You ready to head out?"

"Absolutely," Skyler said enthusiastically, and he was kind of surprised that her apparent disappointment about the museum had dissipated so quickly. "I can't wait to see the ranch."

Skyler had to work to keep up with Hunter; some called her stature petite, but she was just short and her legs always had to work double time to match the stride of a taller person like Hunter. As she walked beside the cowboy, Skyler's mind was whirling with giddy teenage-girl, fantasy-come-to-life thinking.

Hunter Brand!

Even with the bandanna covering the lower part of his face, she had recognized him instantly. Those eyes were unmistakable. She couldn't believe that *the* Hunter Brand, her absolute favorite cowboy on *Cowboy Up!*, was the one to come get her from the airport. She had an entire wall of her bedroom dedicated to Hunter Brand and now he was pushing her luggage cart through the airport? How could her Montana adventure have started any more perfectly? It couldn't have.

She couldn't *wait* to video-chat with her best friend, Molly; Molly had also had a teenage fantasy about marrying Hunter. She was going to lose her mind.

Once outside, Hunter lowered the bandanna and Skyler was able to see his entire handsome face. Yes, he had aged from his time on the show and that age had done him good. The man had a beautifully chiseled jawline, a slight dimple in his chin, prominent cheekbones and a perfectly straight, strong nose. Golden skin, jet-black hair peeking out from beneath his well-worn cowboy hat and just the deepest sapphire-blue eyes. There wasn't any other word that she could think of to describe the grown-up Hunter Brand other than *hunk*.

Hunter dropped the tailgate of his blue Chevy truck and began to toss her baggage into the bed.

"You brought a lot of stuff," her companion said as he hoisted the largest bag into the back of his truck.

"I wasn't sure what to bring," she said, feeling a bit self-conscious over the sheer number of bags she had brought. It did seem excessive now that she was actually here.

Hunter paused and looked at her dead in the face. "For ranch work? Jeans, boots, hat, T-shirts, underwear and plenty of socks."

"Check and check." She made little check marks in the air with a self-effacing laugh.

"I'm not sure you quite understand what you've signed up for here," Hunter said.

It didn't take a genius to read the subtext: Hunter thought she was soft—a real pushover. She could almost hear an unsaid "little lady" hanging in the air between them.

"Don't you worry your pretty little head about me for one second," Skyler said as she picked up one of her medium-size bags. "I can pull my own weight."

Skyler grunted as she attempted to pick up the heavy bag high enough to get it into the truck bed. Unable to get the bag into the truck, and well aware of Hunter's eyes on her, she pushed the bag against the tailgate and squatted down so she could get some leverage. But, even with the extra leverage, she just couldn't get the darn bag into the stupid truck.

"Need a hand?"

Smug.

"Sure. If you want.," she said quickly, trying to cover up how breathless she felt from this simple, mundane task.

With one hand, Hunter easily pushed the bag into the back of the truck. Hunter closed the tailgate with a smirk on his lips.

"Pull your own weight," he said with a deadpan expression. "I can see that."

"I didn't say I could *lift* my own weight, now did I?" Skyler quickly clarified. "No. I don't think I *did* say that."

Once inside the truck, Hunter rolled all of the windows down to let the fresh air into the cab on the way to Sugar Creek.

"I get tired of wearing this mask," she said. "I tested negative. How about you?"

It felt odd to say it, but she felt like it had to be said nonetheless.

"I tested negative a couple of weeks back and other than picking you up today, I haven't seen a soul."

"That must be why you drew the short straw and had to come to the airport to pick me up, huh?"

"I have marching orders to keep you safe while you're at Sugar Creek Ranch. It's a job like any other."

"Do you mind if I take off my mask?" she asked.

"No."

Gratefully, Skyler took off her mask and breathed in the fresh Montana air, unimpeded, for the first time in her life. She glanced over at Hunter; he had slipped the bandanna down from his face. And then she sighed. It was a long, happy sigh. She didn't know if she was sighing because of the beauty of

Montana, the freshness of the air or the handsomeness of Hunter's profile.

Skyler held on to her hat so it wouldn't get blown off and leaned her head out of the window with her eyes closed. She breathed in deeply as the wind rushed over her face, loving the smell of the Montana air.

With another sigh, she sat upright in the seat. "I don't think I've seen a more beautiful view."

Hunter nodded silently.

"And to think you wake up to all of this every day of your life." After several attempts to have a conversation with Hunter, Skyler took the hint and focused on communicating with people who actually *wanted* to talk to her. She called her dad and then Molly. She texted tons of pictures of the Montana landscape and posted them to her social-media pages.

"That's my brother Gabe's spread right there." Hunter startled her by speaking for the first time in thirty minutes. "Little Sugar Creek."

"It's lovely."

Hunter slowed the truck down and turned onto a gravel drive. "And this here is Sugar Creek Ranch."

Skyler could only internally describe the feeling she was having driving onto Sugar Creek property for the first time as similar to waking up on Christmas morning. There was all of the same eagerness and anticipation, and the excitement of knowing that something wonderful was about to be unwrapped.

The rolling pastures were filled with tall grass bending slightly from a balmy late afternoon breeze, and the breathtaking mountains looked like a living postcard. It was heavenly. It was...

"Holy cow!" Skyler was jerked to the side a bit, her hat falling askew on her head when Hunter hit a huge pothole.

"The rain has just torn this road all to pieces," Hunter explained, swerving to avoid another pothole. "We've got an order of crush and run coming in the next couple of weeks."

"Crush and run?"

"Crushed-up rock to fill in the potholes."

"Oh."

Hunter glanced over at her. "That might just be one of your first jobs. Dragging the crush and run."

Skyler reached for the dashboard to stabilize her body with one hand and hold on to her hat with the other; the truck was bobbing and weaving around so much that she actually began to feel a bit seasick.

"Whatever you need me to do, I will do it." Skyler closed her eyes and fought the feeling of seasickness.

"You okay over there?" She heard Hunter ask the question as he thankfully pulled off the main, pothole-riddled road onto a less bumpy drive.

"Yes. Just a touch of benign positional vertigo, is all. Nothing to worry about." She kept her eyes tightly closed.

Hunter slammed on the brakes in a way that made

Skyler wonder if he was deliberately making her problem worse. The truck jerked to a halt, which made her head snap back against the headrest, and her hat fell forward over her face.

"We're here," he said.

Skyler pushed up the brim of her hat so she could see her summer home-away-from-home. Off the main road, they had driven through a canopy of trees to an opening. Tucked away in the woods there was a private oasis with rustic storage buildings, a horse stable, pastureland and a quaint cabin complete with a front porch and rocking chairs.

"This is mine?"

"Yep." Hunter hopped out of the truck.

"All mine?"

"All yours."

"For the whole summer?" She opened the passenger door, her eyes darting from one spot to another. She had grown up in the city; she loved it and was accustomed to sharing a small amount of square footage with a large amount of people. She had never imagined having this much square footage all to herself.

"This—" she pushed the door slowly shut behind her "—is amazing. Truly amazing."

Hunter was already hauling her bags out of the back of his truck; he seemed like he was in a hurry to be rid of her. It stung a little that *the* Hunter Brand hadn't immediately fallen head over heels for her, as per her thousands of teenage fantasy reels she had played in her head. But that disappointment was overtaken by the sheer beauty all around her. If she had any doubt about her decision to come to Montana so soon after she'd been given the "all clear for now" by her team of doctors, those doubts were gone. This part of the world, so quiet and peaceful, filled with the scent of pine in the air, was exactly the place she needed to be to fully recover. This was somewhere she could build her strength, emotionally and physically.

Skyler wanted to explore the grounds and take some pictures for her friends, but followed Hunter's lead instead and tugged one of her suitcases out of the bed of the truck. She let it land on the ground with a thud and then dragged it behind her. The suitcase wheels hit some rocks and twigs along the way, tipping the bag sideways. By the time she reached the porch steps, she was winded, perspiring and a little bit dizzy. She forced herself not to show on the outside how weak she was feeling on the inside. Her pride wanted to hide her vulnerability from Hunter; not that she should care what her teenage crush thought about her…and yet, she kind of did. Kind of.

Grunting and pulling and bracing her legs so she could tug the suitcase to the top of the steps before Hunter returned to find her, once again, struggling, Skyler finally managed to drag the bag onto the porch. For a moment, she closed her eyes and caught her breath. Lord have mercy, the surgery and chemo had sapped her completely of her stamina and strength.

Without a word, Hunter came over, scooped up the bag at her feet, lifted it onto his shoulder like a sack of potatoes and went back into the cabin. Skyler followed him inside and watched as he dropped her last bag unceremoniously on top of her other bags he had stacked in the living room near an antique wood-burning stove.

"Your family keeps this cabin for guests like me?" It was cozy and woodsy with shiplap walls, a vaulted ceiling in the living room and overstuffed furniture perfect for curling up for a nap. There was a small kitchen off the living room—a little outdated but clean and functional.

"There's never been a guest like you before."

"You've never had a guest like me before?" Skyler ran her hands across the hand-carved, butcher-block countertop.

"No." Hunter adjusted his hat on his head. "You're the first."

As if to indicate he was finished with that topic, he turned his body slightly away from her and pointed down the hallway. "Bedroom. Bathroom. If you like TV you're out of luck. Jock installed a hot spot." Hunter pointed to a device on the counter. "Password is on the back."

"Okay," Skyler said quietly, her mind still stuck on the idea that the Brand family had never had a guest like her before.

"I stocked the fridge with some staples—the vegetables we grow on site, so there's always more where that came from. We can go into town tomorrow and pick up anything else you think you might need."

Hunter stood with his hands on his hips for a minute, looked around for a second and then nodded toward the front door. "Let me take you on a quick tour outside before I go."

Skyler trailed behind him, through the front door, down the porch steps, still mulling over the fact that she was the *first*.

"So, is this *your* cabin?" She had a horrible feeling in her gut that she had displaced him from his own home.

"No," Hunter replied. "This was my brother Liam's cabin. All of us have a stake on the ranch. This is his. He's out at the Triple K Ranch with his wife, Kate. He still keeps his old trucks in this shed right here." He indicated one of the buildings. "So you might see him out here working on them."

"What's in there?" Skyler pointed to a large building next to the garage.

"My brother Shane built an obstacle course in there."

"Wow," Skyler said. "That's impressive."

"Yeah," Hunter agreed. "Shane was a sergeant in the army. He recreated a lot of the obstacles they had in boot camp."

"My father was a gunnery sergeant in the marines."

For the first time, Hunter looked at her with a modicum of interest. "Is that right?"

She nodded. "He worked on tanks and amphibious vehicles."

"Jock had me move some of the horses down from the main barn for your use."

"I have *horses*?"

"Yes." Hunter walked quickly toward the barn. "Jock was under the impression that you can ride."

Two summers at Circle F Dude Ranch were about to come in handy.

"I know my way around a barn," she said confidently.

"Good," he said tersely. "Because starting tomorrow, these two horses are your responsibility for the rest of the summer."

"Why start tomorrow when we have today right now?"

Her comment stopped him in his tracks for a moment. "If you're ready to get to work, there's always work to do."

"I'm ready to work."

She was exhausted and already sweaty under her

clothes; the wig was hot and she hated it. But tomorrow waited for no woman.

Something akin to respect flashed in Hunter's striking blue eyes. They were even deeper and bluer in person than they ever had been on TV or in pictures.

"You might want to change into some work clothes then," he advised over his shoulder as he headed toward the barn.

She gave up trying to match his pace, wanting to save some sliver of energy for the barn work. She could collapse totally and completely after Hunter left. "These *are* my work clothes."

They entered the barn, which was old and felt "left behind." There were layers of dust on overturned buckets, and dried-out currycombs left on a tack trunk between the stalls. The wash rack had a layer of hay and dirt plugging the drain; there were cobwebs in almost every corner. The barn could be cleaned up with a little effort and elbow grease. Most important were the beautiful creatures that had been brought to the barn just for her.

"This here is Zodiac." Hunter's tone was much gentler when he was with the horses. The tall chestnut-brown horse with a black mane and tail whickered at them and then nibbled at Hunter's shirt.

"Hi, Zodiac." Skyler let the horse smell her hand. "You are so handsome."

"He's a great cow pony." Hunter gave the horse a pat on the neck. "He'll take care of you out there."

Skyler nodded as if she understood his meaning, but she wasn't sure what Hunter meant by "out there." No doubt she would find out soon enough.

"And this sweet girl is Dream Chaser." Hunter smiled affectionately at the mare across the aisle from Zodiac. "She's as pretty as they come and as sure-footed on the trail as any I've known."

"Hi, Dream Chaser." Skyler pet the mare's neck. She was smaller and stockier than Zodiac, with bright blue eyes and a white blaze on her face, with a brown body and white on her legs.

"I brought a couple of bales of hay down from the main barn just to hold them over. We'll go get more tomorrow and load up the feed room."

"Okay." It seemed like Hunter intended to just fold her right into the work at the ranch, and that suited her just fine.

Hunter disappeared out the back of the barn and returned with a wheelbarrow, a pitchfork and a shovel.

"If you grab the manure, I'll get the urine." He handed her the pitchfork.

The old pitchfork was constructed of wood and steel, and it was a whole lot heavier than it looked. When she took it in her hands, the unanticipated weight of it made her lower her hands a bit before she lifted it.

If he noticed her struggling with the pitchfork, he didn't show it. They mucked the stalls and gave the two horses some hay and feed. Then Hunter showed her how to get water from the garage over to the barn.

"I hooked up this hose for the time being." Hunter tugged on the heavy hose to pull it into the barn. "I'm not sure what's wrong with the water pipes in here—I'll have to look in to it later—but for now, this will work." He stopped just inside the barn, turned on the water and let it stream out onto the gravel in front of the barn. "Make sure you let the water run for a while—the sun heats up the hose and you don't want to be giving the horses hot water in their buckets."

By the time they dumped the stall pickings in a compost pile, Skyler didn't have a dry spot on her body. Every crevice was soaked with sweat. Her new boots had been christened with horse manure and mud, her clothes were stuck to her skin, and yet, she felt elated. Exhausted and elated. It had taken all of her mental and physical strength to finish the chores, but she had persevered. She hadn't given up, and she was proud of herself.

"I've got jobs waiting on me," Hunter said at the bottom of the porch steps. "I'll see you tomorrow first thing."

Skyler leaned against the porch railing as much for stability as comfort.

"Hunter?" She said his name to get his attention.

He turned back to her, his eyebrows raised slightly with a question.

"Why do you think Jock agreed to let me come?" She was still stuck on the idea that it wasn't typical for the Brand family to have guests like her at the ranch. With everything going on in the world, why would Hunter's father agree to it?

Hunter repositioned his hat on his head. "You'll have to ask him that yourself, Skyler. Jock didn't ask for my permission and he didn't factor in my opinion to his final decision."

"So you don't think I should be here." She posed it more as a statement of obvious fact rather than a question. She could read his behavior toward her easy enough.

"We aren't a dude ranch," Hunter said matter-of-factly. "My number is on the refrigerator. If you need me, text me."

Skyler crossed her arms in front of her body. "I will. Thank you."

Right before he climbed behind the wheel of his truck, he said, "Get some rest, Skyler. The day starts before dawn and doesn't end until after dark."

Chapter Two

Skyler's first night in the cabin was not ideal. The early evening had been filled with exploration, some unpacking, foraging in the refrigerator and finally talking on the phone while rocking on the front porch. As dusk gave way to night, the realization that she was out in the middle of nowhere began to set in. Other than the small light over the barn, there wasn't any light illuminating the buildings surrounding the cabin. There were a couple of lights on the cabin facing out toward the yard, but the range was very small. Beyond that light, complete and total darkness. And, in the darkness, odd noises that made her feel like a sitting duck. There were predators out there, she was sure of it. Even her total exhaustion from the day of travel and barn work couldn't overtake her nervousness. She dozed off for an hour or two, but would awaken the moment there was a howl or scratching noise or thump on the roof.

She had barely dozed off for the fourth time when loud banging on her front door sent her shooting upright in bed. Her heart was racing and she felt the awful feeling of adrenaline pumping all over her body.

"Skyler!" Hunter yelled. "Time to go to work!"

She cursed, threw off the covers, jumped out of bed and stubbed her toe on the nightstand while she fumbled to turn on the light. She found her phone turned it on and read with fuzzy eyes that is was just after four in the morning.

More banging on her door only served to make her more anxious as she hopped on one leg to pull on her jeans. She snatched the wig off the bedpost and managed to get it onto her head.

"Skyler!"

"Lord, you are an annoying man." Skyler had one sock on and one sock off as she raced to the bathroom to find her wayward bra.

"I'm coming!" she shouted at the top of her lungs. "Stop banging on the door!"

More knocking.

Somehow Skyler managed to get into her bra and pull on a T-shirt; she checked her reflection in the mirror only to realize that the wig was askew.

"Lovely."

She fixed the wig, then picked up her boots on the way to the door. "I swear, if you do not stop banging on my door, I will…"

Skyler tried to open the door, but had too many things in her hands, so she dropped the sock and boots, unlocked the door and the yanked it open.

"Good morning," Hunter said nonchalantly.

"Good morning?"

"That's what I said."

Skyler scooped up her boots and sock and walked over to the couch, leaving the door open and Hunter standing in the doorway.

"It's not even five o'clock in the morning," Skyler complained while she pulled on her other sock. "It's not even light outside yet."

"I told you we start before dawn around here."

"I heard you." She pushed her foot into a boot. "I thought it was a metaphor."

For the first time, Hunter actually smiled at her, and that smile almost made it worth it to be up at this ungodly hour. The straight white teeth and the dimples sucked her right back in to her teenage fantasy crush.

What a hunk. An annoying hunk. But a total hunk nonetheless.

"A metaphor for what?" he asked.

"I don't know." She stood up and stomped her foot into her boot; her hair fell into her face and she threw it over her shoulder, irritated. "Life."

"No. I was giving you the facts of life here on the ranch."

There was a moment of silence in the room that broken by the sound of her stomach loudly growling.

"I need to grab something to eat," she said, stating the obvious.

"Critters first."

"Critters first?" she repeated. "Meaning?"

"The animals can't feed themselves. You eat after they eat."

"Oh." She frowned. "How many are in the buffet line ahead of me?"

Another dimpled smile. "Hundreds."

Not wanting to give him the opportunity to milk one more ounce of enjoyment out of her apparent misery, Skyler grabbed an apple out of the refrigerator, then got her phone and her hat, and joined him on the porch.

"Ready."

Hunter checked his watch. "You're late."

"How can I be late when *you* didn't tell me what time to be ready?" She trotted after him.

He flipped on the light in the barn aisle. "I said before dawn. It's before dawn."

"Well." She smiled at the image of Zodiac and Dream Catcher blinking their eyes sleepily in the light, their heads hanging low over the stall gate. "Maybe we could drill down on a specific time for tomorrow. Maybe *that* would be helpful."

"Sure," Hunter said in an uncharacteristically agreeable tone of voice. "Let's drill down on, let's say, four a.m. every day."

Skyler's shoulders slumped. "Every morning?"

He handed her a large plastic scoop. "Fill this with feed to the top and then split it between the two of them. After they're done eating, they can go out to the pasture."

She looked at the scoop in her hand.

"And, yes," he added, "every morning. Unless, of course, you think that the horses could do without eating one day so you can have a spa day."

Skyler talked back to him in her head, thinking of all sorts of snarky things she could say in response. But in reality, she zipped her lip, fed the horses and sprayed them both with fly spray, glad that she had muscle memory from summer camp, and then haltered each horse and took them out to the adjacent pasture. The moon was still in the sky; it was still completely dark outside.

"That wasn't too bad. What's next?" she asked with her most cheerful, perky, you-can't-get-me-down voice.

"Follow me."

"You know how to drive a tractor?" Hunter asked his shadow.

"Sure," Skyler said evenly. "That's how I get to work every morning. Tractor."

He found himself smiling again, but had his back to her so she couldn't see it. Skyler, he had quickly discovered, shared his caustic wit and tendency to be a smart-ass. Yet another thing he liked about the tourist.

"Hop up there," Hunter said.

Skyler climbed into the tractor seat and looked around to familiarize herself with the different components; she would have to scoot forward in order to reach the pedals, but other than that, it was a pretty comfortable seat.

"First, you'll want to..." Hunter began.

Skyler moved the gear to Neutral, stepped on the clutch, turned the key to first notch, waited for a red light to come on and then after the red light went off, she cranked the engine.

"...move the gear into Neutral, step on the clutch, wait for the glow light to..." Hunter stopped talking and started watching.

She sent him a pleased grin. "After the Marines, Dad opened a garage and worked on plenty of diesel engines. I haven't driven a tractor, but I have driven a semi."

"Well..." Hunter said slowly, "I'll be damned."

A sliver of light from the sun rising up behind the far-off mountains was glowing pink as Hunter hopped into the trailer hitched to the tractor.

"Put her in gear and drive up this path." Hunter sat down on top of the bales of hay stacked in the tractor. "We'll feed this herd first and then move on to the next."

For the next several hours, they worked together. Rain had been scarce so they were throwing hay in the fields to keep the cows well-fed. It was tedious work, but Skyler enjoyed it. Her misery from lack of sleep and being up early was overshadowed by the sound of cows mooing for their breakfast and the feeling of purpose that driving the tractor had given her. They finished with the cows and then Hunter directed her to drive the tractor to a field of horses.

"Watch this," Hunter said after she drove the tractor through the open gate. He closed the gate behind them, hopped back on the trailer and then whistled loudly.

Now the sun was sending off a soft yellow glow over the rolling hills before her. And then, off in the distance, faint at first, was the sound of pounding. Then she saw them—a herd of horses galloping in the horizon. They were whinnying and kicking up their heels, their ears forward, their necks arched, legs pumping as they raced across the field.

Skyler was mesmerized by the sight; it was if she was seeing horses in the wild, because they were so free. It moved her to tears.

"I have never seen anything that beautiful before."

"It never gets old," Hunter mused.

He directed her to drive toward the herd, to meet

them at their target—the row of black rubber food bowls.

As the herd approached, the horses began to start vying for the first bowl of feed, pinning their ears back, nipping and kicking.

"Is this safe?" Skyler asked, recalling that the Circle F Dude Ranch hadn't taught her how to handle this scenario.

"Not necessarily." Hunter waved a flag at the herd to back them off from the food bowls. He kept them at bay with the flag as she drove slowly from bowl to bowl, dumping grain. They also dropped bales of hay for the herd before they headed back to her cabin.

"The rest of the hay will go into your barn."

"And then can I eat?" she asked, her stomach hurting from lack of food.

"Then we can eat." As she drove through the gate he had opened for her, Skyler caught a quick smile on the cowboy's face. He was so darn handsome when he smiled.

He directed her while she backed the trailer close to the barn and then she switched off the engine. The bales of hay weighed nearly fifty pounds each and, try as she might, she couldn't lift one bale by herself.

"I've got this." Hunter picked up the bale she had dragged off the back of the trailer. "Do a quick check and make sure they still have water in the pasture."

"Are you sure?" Skyler asked, winded.

"Yeah. Go check on the water and then get your-self some chow." He carried the bale of hay toward the feed room. "We've got a pasture fence to tear down after breakfast."

On her way to check the water, Skyler took her finger and itched beneath the wig. This was an idea she hadn't really thought through; farm work wearing a wig just wasn't practical. It was still early morning—she wouldn't even be at her desk job at this hour back home—and she was already sweat-ing through her clothes, and her real hair and scalp were soaked beneath the wig. And it itched!

She was half-tempted just to yank off her wig at breakfast and be done with it. The horses thankfully had water, so she wouldn't have to fight the hose to pull it over to the trough. That was a lucky break. She made it to the porch steps and had to sit down.

"Lord, give me strength." Skyler rested her head in her hands. She closed her eyes and let her body enjoy the moment of rest. It was going to take all of her will to keep up with Hunter, but it was also forc-ing her to build up her stamina more quickly than if she had been at home.

"You okay?" Hunter had finished the chore of stocking the barn with hay; he was brushing the loose pieces of hay off his clothing and arms when he came upon Skyler slumped forward on the front steps of the porch, her head in her hands.

She didn't raise her head. "I'm okay."

He didn't believe her for a second and there was a part of him that knew he had pushed her too hard on her first morning. He knew it because it had been deliberate.

After a second or two of mulling, Hunter extended his hand to her. First and foremost, he had been raised to be a gentleman by his mother, Lilly.

"Let's go rustle up some grub," Hunter said. "I'll show you how to make a real cowboy breakfast."

It took a moment, but Skyler tilted her head up, saw his offered hand and slowly slipped her small hand into his. The bones of her hand were so delicate to the touch that he mentally warned himself not to hold on to her fingers to tightly.

When she stood, she swayed slightly and he caught her under the elbow. He felt terrible.

"Let's get you inside."

Skyler put her hand on her forehead and smiled weakly at him. "I'm just a little dehydrated, I think. I'm not used to sweating so much before it's even noon."

He helped her sit down at the kitchen counter and got her a glass of water. "Just sit there and cool off."

Hunter grabbed some of their ranch-fresh eggs out of the refrigerator, put a skillet on the stove and found a bowl.

"Breakfast hash okay?"

Skyler nodded, taking several big gulps of the water. Her skin had a chalky hue and her eyes looked sunken in her oval face. She didn't look well.

"I'm sorry," Skyler said in a raspy voice.

"No." Hunter frowned, unhappy with his own behavior. He'd been so stuck on the idea of getting rid of her, he'd run her into the ground. "I'm sorry."

Once the skillet was heated, he poured some sunflower oil in the pan, diced some potatoes and onions and threw them in the oil, and then dumped a can of corn-beef hash in the mix.

"That smells good," the tourist said.

"It's gonna be good," he said, frying two eggs sunny-side up. He'd made this meal a hundred times before for his brothers and crew, but never for a lady. But it was the quickest thing he knew how to make in order to get food into her body.

"This will turn you into a cowgirl quicker than anything." Hunter separated the hash onto two plates and then put a fried egg on the top of the hash. He slid the plate her way and then handed her a fork.

"Thank you," Skyler said, loading her fork with eggs and hash.

Hunter sat down next to her at the breakfast bar, hunched over his plate and dug in. He was pretty hungry himself.

"Hmm." He nodded his head when he took his first bite. "One of my better batches."

He looked over at Skyler, who was focused on stuffing as much of the hash into her mouth as she could. Her cheeks were as full as a chipmunk's when she looked up at him, made a happy noise and gave him a thumbs-up.

His companion didn't speak until the majority of her hash was gone. "I've never had this before."

"Do you like it or are you just desperate?" Hunter scooped the last bite of his breakfast onto his fork.

"Both." Skyler followed suit and pushed the last bit of hash onto her fork with her finger. She licked her fingers and then gobbled up the rest of the hash.

Hunter gathered up their plates and put them in the sink while Skyler guzzled down another glass of water. She put down the glass on the counter and he was heartened to see that some of the color had returned to her face.

"Why don't you take the afternoon off?" he suggested.

"Absolutely not." Skyler shook her head. "I feel better now. Tomorrow I need to get up earlier and grab something to eat before you show up at my door, that's all."

"Are you sure?"

"Are you going to rest this afternoon or are you going to work?"

"I'm going to be pulling a fence down."

"Then—" he saw resolve in Skyler's lovely lavender eyes "—I'm going to be pulling a fence down, too."

After breakfast, Skyler excused herself to the bathroom so she could regroup. It really annoyed her to no end that her body, as it had for the last year, had given out on her. Before cancer, she had been tiny but mighty. That's what her father had always said. She hated to feel weak, no matter the cause.

In the bathroom, Skyler pulled off the wig and wet a washcloth, then wiped down her head, scalp, face and neck. She stared at her reflection in the mirror; baby-fine strawberry blond hair had sprouted all over her head. Skyler rubbed her hand over the new growth, grateful to have it at all. But she didn't feel ready to open the topic of her illness with Hunter, so she would just have to find a way to tolerate the heavy, hot wig until she *was* ready.

Skyler put the wig back onto her head, adjusted it and then pushed her cowgirl hat on top of the wig. Honestly, in her mind, she looked one of those L.O.L. Surprise dolls that were so popular with young girls—the wig added extra height to her head, making her face look longer and narrower and her eyes look overly large.

"It's a look." She rolled her eyes at herself before she quit the mirror and left the bathroom.

"Ready?" Hunter was waiting for her outside.

"Ready."

Hunter had her follow him on the tractor while he drove his truck. They headed deeper into Sugar Creek property, heading up a slight incline until they reached a clearing at a plateau. Hunter gestured for her to pull the tractor to the right of where he was parked. He jumped out of his truck and walked over to an old three-railed fence that had been turned a grayish brown by the sun. Many of the rails were broken or split; some of the rails were missing.

"We want to expand this pasture—give the herd some more grazing land to the north."

Skyler rested her arms on the steering wheel of the tractor.

"Where do we begin?" she asked, feeling daunted by the task.

"How do you eat an elephant?" Hunter grabbed some tools out of his truck.

One of her oncologists, Dr. Bryant, always asked her that same question.

"One bite at a time." She swung down off the tractor.

"Exactly."

They worked side by side as the sun beat down on them. Hunter was a quiet worker and so was she. The cowboy would pull off the boards, using a crowbar to wrench them away from the posts, while Skyler did her best to haul the boards to the trailer.

"Do what you can." Hunter was as sweaty as she was. "It's hot and I don't want you to overdo again."

Skyler nodded as she wrapped her arms around the end of a rail and pulled as hard as she could to get it to move a couple of feet. She stopped, dropped it, caught her breath and then picked it up again. Even if she could only haul one board for Hunter, it was better than nothing.

"If you can pull that wire off the boards before I get to the them, that would be a big help." Hunter wiped off his forehead.

Chicken wire had been tacked to the boards to stop the horses from getting their heads stuck in between the planks if they tried to eat greener blades of grass on the other side of the fence. Hunter handed her a hammer.

"Use this to pull the nails out. Keep the nails in your pocket because we don't want them left behind for the horses to step on."

Skyler took the hammer, glad that Hunter had put the earlier episode behind him and was treating her as she wanted to be treated: like an equal.

One by one, Skyler fought with the nails, cursing at times, getting frustrated at times, but also feeling triumphant when she managed to wrench a nail loose and pull a part of the wire away from the post, paving the way for Hunter to do his job.

Skyler locked her fingers into the spaces of the wire, put her boot on the post and then pulled as hard as she could. The wire gave way more quickly than she anticipated and she stumbled backward.

"Careful." Hunter seemed to always be watching her out of the corner of his eye.

She nodded but kept focused on her task. The more she worked, the hotter her scalp became; sweat was rolling down her cheek and the need to itch under the wig only made her feel more frustrated and irritable.

She bent down to take the bottom nail out of the post, and when she did, her hair got tangled up in the wire. When she lifted up her head, it tugged the wig sideways.

"Damn it!" Skyler grabbed the tangled hair and managed to pull it loose, leaving some golden blond strands still wound around the rusty wire.

She stood upright, her fingers balled up into a fist with her free hand, her other hand gripping the handle of the hammer until it hurt.

"Enough!" she said through gritted teeth. "Enough, enough, *enough*!"

Hunter spun around to face her just in time to see her throw her hat on the ground, yank off her wig, throw it down as hard as she could, stomp on it several times, then pick up her hat and plop it back onto her head.

Her breathing labored from the heat and the hissy fit, Skyler stared at Hunter while he stared back at her. They stood for several seconds, just staring at each other, before he asked, "Feel better?"

It took a moment for his question to register—it hadn't been the question she had prepared herself to answer. She breathed in deeply and then laughed as she exhaled. "Yes. Much."

Skyler knew that this wasn't the end of the discussion between them. But Hunter's willingness to keep focused on the job and ignore the fact that she had just pulled off a wig and stomped it into the ground was exactly what she needed.

"Good." Hunter turned back to his task. "Now let's get back to work."

Chapter Three

Pulling down the fence was more than a one-day job. It was like that on the ranch—some jobs took one shot and other jobs lingered on for months before they were finished.

"Let's knock off for now." Hunter stood upright and then stretched to ease the tension in his back. "It's about time for lunch."

Skyler was wrestling with a plank of wood, dragging it toward the trailer.

"Okay," his helper grunted. "Just let me get this last board on the trailer."

Hunter walked over to where she was struggling and picked up the other end of the plank. Then they carried it together the rest of the way. Together, they lifted it up and dropped it onto the trailer.

"Thank you." Skyler kneeled down in her spot. "That was tough."

"You did real good," Hunter said. "Better than I would've thought."

Skyler didn't move. While she caught her breath, he pulled some cold bottles of water out of a cooler in the bed of his truck. He twisted off the cap of one and offered it to her.

"Drink this."

Skyler stood up, her shoulders slumped forward and her face beet-red, and took the bottle from him. She guzzled the water down almost in one gulp, breathing in deeply after she was finished.

"Thank you," she said again, sitting down on the edge of the trailer.

Hunter was very proud of Montana and the women who were raised here. He had always believed that the women of Montana had certain qualities—strength, gumption and perseverance—that women from other parts of the country didn't have. It was a tough life, and he had seen, time and again, the women in his life step up to the plate and work side by side with the men to keep the ranch running. Skyler had earned his respect today; no matter how tired she was, how out of breath, frustrated or angry, she never stopped moving forward. She never stopped trying.

"My hat is too big now," Skyler complained,

pushing her cowgirl hat back on her head. "It fit just fine when I had the wig on."

Hunter hadn't known how to react about the wig, so he hadn't reacted at all. He'd just kept on working like he had been trained to do all his life. "Focus on the job, son," his father always said. But while his hands were busy working, his mind had been working overtime, too. The shorn hair wasn't a fashion statement for Skyler—she had been sick. And the discovery, even though he hadn't shown any reaction to Skyler, was a kick in the gut. Old memories of a friend long gone and sorely missed felt like someone had ripped out stitches and reopened a wound not yet healed. Now, at least, he understood why Jock was so insistent that Skyler be allowed to have her ranch-life experience.

"I'll see if my sister has an extra hat you can borrow. I bet you're the same size."

Skyler was staring hard at the discarded wig; the wig was covered in dust and dirt, and had been trampled on several times while she hauled wood to the trailer.

Not looking at him, Skyler asked, "Why haven't you asked me about it?"

Hunter finished off his own water, squinted at the sun and said, "Folks in these parts don't go around asking too many questions. We figure if you want us to know something, you'll tell us sooner or later.

And if you don't, then it wasn't any of our business to begin with."

She looked up at him, and once again, he was temporarily mesmerized by the goodness he saw in those wide, violet-blue eyes. What he saw in those eyes was a heart of gold, a kind soul and a woman who had seen more than her fair share of hardship. In that instant, he realized that he had been wrong about her from the get-go. She wasn't a spoiled socialite playing dress-up; she was a woman on a mission to save her own life through the hard work and fresh air that could be found on a Montana ranch.

"Let's head back and grab some lunch," Hunter said. "You up for driving the tractor back?"

Skyler stood up slowly, her hat falling forward over her eyes. With a frustrated noise in the back of her throat, she pushed the hat up so she could see.

"I'm up for it," she said and headed toward the tractor, leaving the wig half buried in the dirt.

"I feel human again." Hunter leaned back in the rocking chair, his booted feet up on the porch railing.

"Me, too," Skyler sighed happily.

They had returned to her cabin and made sandwiches for lunch. She hadn't fully regained her appetite before she'd left for Montana, but now it was coming back with a vengeance. She had eaten two whole sandwiches and three glasses of fresh-squeezed lemonade that Hunter's sister-in-law Savannah had made specially ahead of her arrival. It had been the right amounts of tartness and sweetness, and she had greedily guzzled as much as her stomach would allow.

They sat in silence together; it was a comfortable silence, which Skyler didn't often experience. She was typically a nervous talker, always wanting to fill in the silences if her mind wasn't focused on a task. But with Hunter, silence was easy. After a while, Skyler felt ready to talk, ready to fill in some of the silence between them.

Not looking directly at him, she said, "I had cancer."

In her peripheral vision, she saw Hunter look her way. "Had?"

"Yes." A nod. "Had."

"Good news that you can use the past tense."

"Great news, really." Skyler rocked back and forth in the chair. "This trip to Montana was motivation for me."

There was a long pause before Hunter asked, "Is that right?"

"My best friend, Molly, she's the one who arranged the whole thing," Skyler explained. "She knew that I have dreamed of Montana my whole entire life. It started out as a bucket-list trip, but then it became a celebratory trip. My friends and co-workers, family—they started a GoFundMe page so I could fly private out here. I had strangers donate, too," she said with wonder in her voice. "Can you believe that? People who've never met me pitched in so I could get out here safely during the pandemic."

"People can surprise you."

"Absolutely they can," she agreed. "Your father surprised all of us by not canceling."

She saw a muscle work in Hunter's jaw and she almost thought that he had something that he wanted to say on that subject—something he might want to add—but when he kept silent, she thought she must have been mistaken.

"Either way, I'm here now." She rocked back and forth several times, the heat of the day feeling less taxing under the cool auspices of the porch over-hang. She breathed in deeply, feeling grateful for the day.

"The wig was not one of my better ideas," she admitted, the thought just popping out of her mouth.

Hunter remained silent on the matter.

"I wanted to feel normal when I arrived," she added.

"You don't owe me any explanation," Hunter said.

"It's not really the best way to meet someone— 'Hi, my name is Skyler. I've had a rare form of lung cancer. How you doin'?'"

That made Hunter crack a smile and show those dimples she loved so much.

She turned her body a little toward him. "Now that you know, don't you feel sorry for me!"

"I don't."

"And don't you go easy on me because of it."

This was met with silence.

"Don't you go easy on me because of it," she repeated. "I'm serious. Treat me like you'd never found out."

He looked over at her, squinting a bit. "That's what you want?"

"That's exactly what I want."

"Then that's what you're gonna get."

"Good," she insisted.

"Fine by me."

"Fine by me!" she said more loudly than he did.

That made the dimples come out again. Lord, the man was cute. Sitting on a porch in Montana with Hunter Brand—now this really was her dream coming true. At least the dream she had held dear when she was a teenage girl with braces and a flat chest.

At least the braces were gone.

"So what's next?"

Hunter slipped his hat down over his face and leaned his head back like he was going to take a nap. "After our food digests a bit, I think I want to check out your riding skills. We'll saddle up the horses and go out on the trail."

She hadn't ridden in years, but it had to be like riding a bike, didn't it?

"Sounds like a plan." She titled up her face to

catch the rays of sun that weren't blocked by the porch overhang.

After a minute or two, Hunter asked, "I've been wondering…how *did* your friend know about Sugar Creek? It's a bit off the beaten path, isn't it?"

Skyler's stomach clenched a bit and her nose wrinkled as she winced. Somehow she knew this question was going to arise; she had just hoped to have a little more time with Hunter before having to confess.

"Cowboy Up!"

Hunter dropped his feet from the porch railing and his boots landed on the wooden planks with a loud thud. He leaned forward, repositioned his hat on his head so he could look at her with a hint of accusation in his bright, ocean-blue eyes.

"I *knew* you recognized me from the show," he said. "I *knew* it."

"Guilty as charged," she admitted. "But what I said at the airport wasn't a lie exactly. I *did* recognize you from the website. I just *also* recognized you from the show."

Hunter didn't sit back in his chair; his shoulders seemed tense as she watched him wipe his hand over his face. He didn't look at her when he asked, "Please tell me you aren't part of one of those fan clubs online."

She laughed. "I promise you. I'm not."

He let out a relieved breath. "Well, that's something, at least."

"Molly and I loved that show," Skyler continued. "We always watched it together. We never missed an episode."

Hunter leaned his elbows on his legs, his head down a bit. "I'm glad you got some pleasure out of it. But agreeing to do that show was the worst mistake of my life. I've wished I could go back a million times and get a do-over. But I can't."

"Really?" Her eyebrows furrowed. "Why? You were great on the show."

Skyler stopped herself from gushing about the countless hours she binge-watched marathon showings of *Cowboy Up!* just to see him ride a horse or sit around a campfire playing guitar with his friends. And she sure as heck wasn't going to confess the many daydreams she had had about marrying him. Judging by his reaction, that secret was best kept in the vault.

Hunter sat back again, seeming to relax. "Being famous isn't what it's cracked up to be, especially if you want to be taken seriously as a rancher in a small town."

Up until that moment, Skyler hadn't realized that she had only been seeing Hunter as a one-dimensional character from a TV show instead of a flesh-and-blood man. It had never occurred to her that *Cowboy Up!* had been anything but amazing for Hunter.

After all, being a part of his life, vicariously through the show, had been so amazing for her.

She sought to lighten the mood and set him at ease. "Well, I promise that I'm not a stalker. Just a fan."

"Good to know."

She stared at his profile. "But I do have some posters and T-shirts that I would like for you to sign."

Hunter shot up again, his brow furrowed. "Are you serious?"

"No." She shook her head with a smirk. "I was just teasing you."

"You really spooked my mule, Skyler," he said, the dimples coming out. Then he stood up and raised his arms over his head in a stretch. For the briefest of moments, his button-down shirt raised up, revealing strong, defined abs—the kind that tempted the touch. "All right. Enough resting. You ready to go for a ride?"

She didn't want to let on, but she could do with some more rest. Honestly, she felt as if she had already done weeks' worth of work before lunch and the conversation had tired her out even more.

"Sure," Skyler said with a weak smile. "Lead the way."

At first, when she tried to stand up her legs didn't want to cooperate. She fell back a bit and then tried again. Hunter had his back to her and didn't notice, which suited her just fine. She pushed herself upright, reaching for the railing. In a split second, her world narrowed and the edges of her vision closed in around her. She heard herself say Hunter's name and then everything around her faded to black.

"Why didn't you tell me she was sick?" Hunter whispered harshly into the phone.

"It was her business to tell, not mine," Jock said in his terse manner. "What's going on now?"

"Well, she damn well passed out, Dad." He rested one hand on the porch railing. "I worked her like a man before I even knew anything was wrong."

"You should've eased her in, regardless," his father admonished. "That's just good sense, son."

Yes, it would have been good sense if he hadn't been determined to send her packing back to the city. It would have been good sense if he had a clue that Skyler had health concerns. He didn't have a decent argument so he just moved on.

"Does she need to go to the hospital?"

"I tried to take her and she refused to go. She's resting now," he said. "I think she just got overheated and overly tired."

"Well, that's on you, son. Keep me posted," Jock said. "And let her know we're planning a family get-together—outdoors so everyone can be safe. We all want to make her feel welcome even though we've got this *pan-dammit* going on."

"Yes, sir." Hunter nodded. "I'll do that."

"Take care of her as if she were one of our own, Hunter. I wouldn't expect any less of you."

He ended the call with his father, put his phone in his back pocket and then stared out at the landscape. Jock had pulled the perfect bait and switch on him. He had thought he was getting a bratty city girl who flew around on private jets wasting people's time for kicks. She was in Montana chasing a dream; she was in Montana to regain her life and her health.

The door opened to the cabin while his mind was wandering and he was staring out at the field. He turned to find Skyler standing in the doorway, looking smaller and slighter than before, but the color had returned to her face.

"That was terrible." Skyler had her arms crossed and she sounded, to his ears, embarrassed.

"Do you feel well enough to sit down out here with me?" he asked.

Arms still crossed, she nodded. She sat down in the chair she had occupied earlier. This time she curled her legs up to her chest and wrapped her arms around them.

"I'm sorry I pushed you so hard, Skyler." Hunter was seeking her forgiveness. He had acted like a class-A jerk and he knew it.

"This isn't your fault," she said quickly, emphatically. "I wanted to keep up, show you that I wasn't going to be a burden to you this summer…"

"I didn't want you here, so I made it tougher on

you than it needed to be." Hunter decided to just clear the air between them. He felt like he owed her that much.

"I know that." Skyler met his gaze. "And I wanted to prove you wrong. Instead, I made your point for you."

"No. You didn't. Everyone needs time to acclimate to this kind of work. I ran you ragged and for that I'm sorry. I want you to accept my apology."

"I do."

"Good. Thank you. Now we can start over." Hunter was surprised that she'd forgiven him so easily, so willingly, so completely. He had just told her that he had deliberately run her down and she had nothing but acceptance and friendship in her eyes, which could only be described as lavender with flecks of blue and gray. Lovely eyes. Perhaps the most beautiful he had ever seen. In fact, at times, he found it difficult to break the gaze…to look away from those eyes.

Skyler smiled sweetly at him, yawned and then her eyes drooped down. "I think I'm going to go lie down again. What time should I expect you tomorrow?"

"Let's make is seven." Hunter stood up with her.

"What about the horses, the cows?" she asked, worried.

"I've got them. You just get some rest and we'll go for that trail ride before it gets too hot."

Skyler nodded in agreement as she headed to the front door.

"By the way," Hunter said, "Jock is planning a family cookout. Outside—plenty of social distancing. Everyone wants to meet you."

Skyler smiled that sweet smile at him again. "And I very much want to meet them."

"It's been more than I hoped for." Skyler was propped up in bed video-chatting with Molly. Molly's friendly, pretty face was a comfort to her and she was grateful to Jock for ensuring that she had a solid internet connection in her little private oasis on the ranch. Molly's father was a redheaded Irishman and her mother was a doctor from Haiti; with those genetics, Molly had inherited long, curly sable hair, moss-green eyes and darker skin with the most endearing freckles across the bridge of her nose and cheeks. And her dear friend had the best smile of anyone she had ever known.

"Everyone has loved the pictures you've been posting," her friend said from her micro patio. In the city, Molly's minuscule outdoor space was considered a luxury.

"I've been trying to be kind of low-key about all of the pictures. Hunter doesn't like for his picture to be taken and he definitely doesn't like social media."

"Hunter." Molly put her hand over her heart, fluttered her long, curled eyelashes and pretended to faint.

"Hunter," Skyler repeated in a dreamy voice. "He's so handsome in person, you wouldn't believe it. But, you know…he's better than I had imagined. Nicer."

Molly's eyes widened. "What if you actually marry Hunter Brand? Just think about it. All of those mock weddings we produced between Hunter and you would actually be dress rehearsals!"

That made Skyler laugh. "No. I don't think marriage between Hunter and me is written in the stars. When he first saw me, he looked at me like I was an alien from Mars."

"Well, that wig was odd."

Skyler laughed harder. "I know it was. You tried to tell me."

"Good riddance."

"Agreed," she said. "But now that he knows I've been sick, he treats me like his little sister." She rolled her eyes. "It's *whatever.*"

"Well, I think Hunter Brand would be crazy *not* to fall in love with you."

"Thank you." She smiled; Molly was always there to lift her spirits. "I wish you were here with me. It's like walking on to the set of *Cowboy Up!* The family is going to have an outdoor get-together in a couple of weeks. I'm looking forward to that. By that time, I think all of the quality time with trees and solitude will be getting old."

"I wonder if Chase will be there."

Chase Rockwell was one of Hunter's friends and another dream-worthy cowboy on *Cowboy Up!* Molly had always had a hard time choosing between Chase and Hunter. For Skyler, it had never been a contest: it had always been Hunter. In fact, it still was.

"I don't think so. Hunter says the ranch has been closed up pretty tightly—only essential workers have been coming in."

"And one pretty little redhead." Molly grinned at her.

"I did manage to slip through the cracks, didn't I?"

"It was meant to be," her friend reiterated. "Hey. I've got to run. Make sure you ask Hunter about Chase. Neither one of them are on social media. Find out if he's married!"

Skyler hung up with her friend and slipped out of bed. Alone in the woods, she felt comfortable stepping outside without a bra on. She pulled on a ribbed tank top, a clean pair of jeans and her newly christened dusty boots.

On the front porch, she pulled in a deep breath and then let it out slowly. It was late afternoon and the air was still. Other than some birds chirping and fluttering from one tree limb to another, it was quiet. Slowly, carefully, Skyler made her way down

the porch steps, still feeling wobbly from her earlier ordeal.

Across the yard, she made her way to a giant
boulder at the edge of the clearing near the gravel
drive that led back to the main ranch road. Skyler
had been pulled toward this boulder since she had
first spotted it. This was the perfect perch for her
daily meditation. When she reached the boulder, she
ran her hands over the smooth surface; it was covered with swirls of gold and black and white. It had
small crevices and places where tiny wildflowers
were trying to grow.

Skyler found a foothold and climbed her way to
the top of the boulder. There she sat cross-legged,
hands resting in her lap, her eyes closed, her chin
tilted upward. She wasn't sure how the summer was
going to unfold, but she knew that she was in the
right place at the right time. She felt it in her gut. As
the sun began to set behind her, Skyler began her
gratitude ritual, something she had begun during
the darkest days of her illness. She sat silently, her
body still, and thought of all of her many blessings.
Her list of gratitude was a living document; she was
always adding to it.

"I am grateful for Jock Brand for allowing me to
heal in this most beautiful place. I am grateful for
Hunter Brand, who caught me when I was about
to fall."

Chapter Four

It wasn't how she would have wanted it, but it took her four days to regain her strength. Hunter refused to let her help with the barn chores, only letting her keep him company while he mucked the stalls and occasionally letting her drive the zero-turn lawn mower. It was something she had learned to use with her father when she was young, and she mowed around the cabin and the other buildings. By the fourth day, she was starting to get restless and she told him as much.

"I feel better." She marched after him as he took a load of manure to the compost pile. "Look at me."

Hunter tipped over the wheelbarrow, dumping the contents onto the pile. "I see you."

"I need to get back to work or I'm going to lose my ever-loving mind," she said, irritated. "I'm not some delicate little baby bird that you have to protect."

"That's not how I see it." The cowboy rolled the wheelbarrow over to the barn and tipped it on its side to rinse it out.

Skyler stomped over to the hose, grabbed it, dragged it over to the dirty wheelbarrow and turned on the water. Hunter made a grab for the hose but she held it away from him with a scowl.

"I'm serious. I didn't come here to convalesce in bed. I've done enough of that. I came here to work, to experience ranch life, and it's your job to give me that experience, isn't that right?"

Hunter's jaw was set and he didn't respond.

"Now, I'm as much to blame for that little episode as you are. More, actually. I knew my body was being pushed beyond its limit and I should have just been straight with you, the consequences be damned."

Skyler finished cleaning the wheelbarrow. Then she shut off the water and threw the hose down on the ground as if to punctuate her words.

"I'm tired of the trees. I want to see some people other than you." Skyler had her hands on her hips. "Take me into town *or* give me the keys to your truck and I'll drive myself."

Hunter stared at her, his arms crossed. She could

almost see the wheels turning inside his brain, trying to figure out his next move with her. What he didn't realize was that *she* was going to determine her next move, not him.

Skyler spun on her heel and simultaneously took her phone out of her pocket. "Fine. I'll get an Uber. Does Uber come out this far? Someone has to come out this far, right? We're still in civilization."

"I don't know what you're so worked up about," Hunter called after her.

She stopped and turned back to him. "I'm *bored*. I've seen the trees, I love the trees, but enough with these particular trees!"

"How about that trail ride?" Hunter asked, still planted in his spot.

"Ah, yes. The elusive, promised trail ride," Skyler snorted back at him.

"Let's go get the horses and saddle them up."

A trail ride seemed a much better prospect than town, except for seeing other human beings. When she had imagined Montana for all of those years, she hadn't thought about how lonely it could be. So much land with so few people—it was an adjustment after spending her entire life living in one of the biggest cities in the world.

"Will we see any signs of life other than birds and cows?" she asked, walking toward him.

"I can take you up to the homestead tour," Hunter said. "I can take you up to the main house, ride you by Bruce and Savannah's place, swing by my stake and then finish at Little Sugar Creek."

They brought the horses in from the pasture; Hunter brushed Zodiac, picked out his hooves and sprayed him with fly spray, while she took care of Dream Catcher. She was pleased with how easily her skills came back from her two summers at horse camp. It was like riding a bike; she could only hope that the *riding* part came back as easily.

"You are such a beautiful girl." Skyler combed Dream Catcher's long forelock so it wasn't in the horse's eyes.

Hunter swung a saddle pad and saddle onto Dream Catcher's back. "She was my sister's rodeo ride for years."

"Your sister doesn't mind me riding her horse for the summer?"

Hunter tightened the girth slowly; Dream Catcher pinned her ears back a bit as the girth tightened around her belly. "She's happy that Dream has a job for the summer. She was over in Australia visiting friends when this whole virus thing happened— she decided to hunker down over there until things calm down."

"I'm sorry I'm not going to get to meet her."

Once the horses had been saddled and bridled, Hunter fit her with a helmet so her head was protected from a potential fall. He gave her a leg up; she swung into the saddle and sat down as gently as she could on Dream Catcher's back. She sat upright and held on to the saddle horn, while Hunter adjusted her stirrups the right length.

"How does that feel?"

"Good." She moved around a little to get the feel of the stirrups and the seat of the saddle. "Comfortable."

The cowboy handed her the reins and then mounted Zodiac. He rode up beside her. "You'll let me know if you need to stop."

"Yes," she promised and she meant it sincerely.

They took a trail that ran behind the cabin; she had walked some of the trail on foot but had never gotten very far. She sat taller in the saddle, feeling more confident in her ability to handle the horse. Along the way, she practiced stopping and backing up and shifting Dream Catcher's direction.

"It *is* like riding a bike!"

"Don't get too cocky," Hunter warned. "An experienced trail horse can spook just as easily as a novice trail horse."

They made their way along the curvy trail, crossing several rock-laden streams and trotting up short hills, which made Skyler laugh with joy. Every now and again, Hunter would hoot and holler, and he told her he was making sure the deer cleared out of their way so their sudden movements wouldn't spook the horses. Skyler joined him in the hooting and hollering, and it felt amazing to yell at the top of her lungs in the middle of Montana.

At the edge of the trail, an expanse of pasture-land and fields provided a picturesque foreground for the main house of Sugar Creek Ranch. Of course, she had seen the main house on the show, but to see it in person, to get perspective on the sheer size of the house in relation to the mountains in the background, was another thing entirely.

"Wow." That was all she could say.

"Dad wanted to make a statement." Hunter had stopped Zodiac where the trail met the open field so she could take in the view.

"The statement is 'I have a boatload of money.'" These words just jumped right out of her mouth before she could reel them back in.

Hunter looked over at her and smiled. "You got the message."

Skyler laughed. "Loud and clear."

"You'll meet my parents next week at the cook-out." He turned his horse to the northeast.

"I'm looking forward to that." The family had planned the event to be two weeks after her arrival, in order to observe a fourteen-day quarantine. She was totally on board, but had no idea how long four-teen days could feel!

They followed the tree line along the open field. In the distance, a small herd of deer appeared—three mothers with their seven babies dotted the hillside.

"I need to get a picture of this." Skyler shifted in the saddle to pull her phone out of her pocket. "Look how precious those babies are!"

Hunter stopped Zodiac close enough to Dream Catcher that he could take a hold of the mare's reins. His big-city tourist did exactly what he expected her to do: take way too many pictures of every stump, leaf and common deer on the ranch.

But that's where his assumptions of his summer charge ended. She was completely unexpected, from her firecracker personality to her ability to take pleasure in every little thing in life that she did. Everything in the world seemed to hold wonder for Skyler; she didn't just see a leaf—she saw the miracle of nature. And it made him see the world around him— the world he took for granted and often saw as an obstacle or a chore—in a different light.

"Wow." Skyler turned that bright smile of hers on him. And when she did, he felt something odd in his gut, and it was a feeling that he just couldn't explain, other than the fact that he'd never quite felt it before.

"Right?" she said.

"What? The deer?"

"Yes." Skyler looked at him like he just didn't get it. "Of course, the deer! Aren't they amazing? I love their spindly legs and their little white tails."

"Not really. They're all over the place. And they break the fences. I am forever repairing fences that they have broken with their...what did you call them? Spindly legs?"

Skyler ignored his complaints as they rode toward the deer; it was interesting seeing the ranch through her eyes. He had always loved this land, but perhaps he had been taking it for granted lately.

"They are tasty, I will say that," he added.

"Oh!" Skyler winced at the thought. "How could you, Hunter?"

He laughed, something he found himself doing around Skyler. "Easily. Cook 'em right up, add a little barbeque sauce. Finger lickin' good."

"I don't like you anymore." She turned her head away from him.

As they approached the small herd, the adults lifted their heads, alert, their large ears pointed in their direction. They stood stock-still for a couple of seconds before they raced toward the trees.

"Look!" his companion whispered harshly. "Look!"

So he did. He did look. And he watched. The adult females were singularly focused on reaching the trees, while the babies ran in circles, playing with each other, frolicking in the tall grass. One by one, the babies realized that the adults were in the trees and scurried after them as fast as their dainty legs would take them. He had seen that image hundreds of thousands of times since he was a young boy, but he couldn't remember just stopping and really watching them. He couldn't remember just stopping and appreciating the unique beauty of the animal.

Skyler turned her face toward him, her eyes shining with happiness and joy. He found himself thinking a lot about the cuteness of Skyler's oval face. The features of her face were refined and petite; her lips were bow-shaped and her nose was small and straight. He had thought, at first, that her eyes were too large for her face, giving her an odd look. But now he thought they were perfect for her. He didn't care about her shorn hair; in fact, the new growth made her resemble a pixie or a sprite. When he looked at her, he found himself wanting to keep right on looking. He supposed her felt about Skyler the way she felt about those deer: he was fascinated.

Up over a hill and down the other side, the homestead of his eldest brother, Bruce, and his wife, Savannah, was visible in the valley. A pack of misfit dogs, all rescued from one place or another by his brother and sister-in-law, came barreling toward them, tails wagging, barking loudly and persistently.

The pack of dogs followed them as they rode toward the house that Bruce had built with his own hands for the love of his life, Savannah. In the field beyond the house, Bruce was on his tractor mowing and he could see Savannah, with her long, wavy bright red hair, working in the garden behind the house. Hunter's niece, Amanda, just shy of her fifth birthday, spotted him in the distance and started to jump up and down and yell his name.

Savannah stood up, saw them and waved her arms. Following her daughter's lead, his sister-in-law left the garden so she could meet them in front of the house.

"Uncle Hunter!" Amanda had a head full of russet-brown curls, greenish-blue eyes and a face as pretty as her mother's.

As usual, Savannah was in jeans, boots, a loose T-shirt and a big, floppy hat to keep the sun off of her neck.

"Hi!" Savannah greeted them. "We were hoping you'd stop by!"

Hunter made quick introductions, wishing he could get down off the horse and give his niece a proper hug.

"It's so nice to meet you," Skyler said.

"Same here," Savannah said. "We've all been real excited to have you here for the summer. Did you have a chance to try the lemonade I made for you?"

"The lemonade!" his companion exclaimed. "I have never tasted anything that good. Thank you so much for making me a pitcher."

"It was my pleasure," his sister-in-law said. "I'll make more anytime you want and send it along with Hunter."

"Uncle Hunter!" Amanda was swinging from his

boot while Zodiac didn't move an inch. "Come and play with me."

Savannah wrangled her daughter. "Come here, wild child. Uncle Hunter can't play right now."

"Why not?" his niece asked with a pout that he found irresistible.

"I'll come and play with you soon," he promised. "I'm going to take her over to meet Bruce and then swing by my place…"

"What place?" Savannah laughed, holding on to her daughter's hands and twirling her in a circle.

"It's rustic," Hunter said.

"Rustic?!" His sister-in-law's voice went way up on the question. "You don't have indoor plumbing! Or a roof! Or walls!"

"Minor details."

She said to Skyler, "It's been a lot of big talk and zero action over there at Hunter's place."

"I've just been waiting for the right woman to come along and then I'll build her a house just like Bruce built for you."

"Well, it's not from a lack of options. You've got to commit, Hunter. Find the right one and commit." Savannah waved them off.

"'Bye, Uncle Hunter!" Amanda ran beside them, her chubby legs pumping furiously. "I love you."

"I love you, Princess Amanda!"

The truth of the matter was that he came from a family of marrying men. Four of his elder brothers were already married and he always wanted to join the ranks of married Brand men. Lately, he had been casually dating the daughter of a rancher who owned the large cattle spread that shared Sugar Creek's entire southern border. Like him, Brandy McGregor had Montana in her blood. She was a cattleman's daughter and understood what that kind of life entailed. She was as pretty as the day was long, with willowy legs, naturally buxom and thick, light brown hair. She had been on the rodeo circuit with him, and even though she had been four years behind him in school, they shared the same tight knit group of friends.

Bruce stopped mowing long enough for Hunter to introduce Skyler and then his older brother went right back to work. Hunter understood it—there was only so much daylight a man was afforded each day and always more work to get done than daylight would allow.

"He's got a lot of field left to cut," Hunter explained.

"I see that." Skyler seemed to be sitting straighter in the saddle, her chin up, her shoulders back.

"You feeling okay or do we need to head back?"

"No. I always want to go forward. Never back. Only forward."

"Wow!" Skyler said. "I really need to come up with a new word to use. But…*wow*."

"Do you like it?"

"Like it? I *love* it! Can we stop and take a look around?"

"We've got the time," Hunter said. "I planned on getting back to the fence tomorrow if the weather holds."

Skyler swung her leg over the saddle, took her foot out of the stirrup and then slid down to the ground. When she landed, her knees ached and she realized that her entire backside was sore. She winced as she straightened up, feeling like she was in her eighties instead of just approaching thirty. Her annoying aches and pains were soon forgotten as her attention was drawn to the stake of Sugar Creek land that Hunter had claimed for his own.

"You can just drop her reins." Hunter walked up beside her. "Dream is trained to ground tie."

Skyler dropped the horse's reins, gave her a pat on her neck and then walked toward the cluster of ancient oak trees at the top of a small hill.

"I call her Oak Tree Hill," Hunter said of his place.

The cluster of hundred-year-old oak trees, with their thick trunks and far-reaching, glorious canopies, beckoned to her. Surrounding the trees was unfenced pastureland lush with grass and indigenous wildflowers. Beneath the trees, the temperature was cooler and the sun was almost entirely blocked.

"Hunter." Skyler stopped beneath one of the oak trees. "This is paradise."

The smile he sent her was different from the others; he appreciated that she loved his spot in the world.

"No one else wanted this spot." Hunter leaned back against one of the trees. "Too far out, too hard to build."

"The harder you have to work, the more you appreciate it." Skyler wandered deeper beneath the tree canopy. "That's what my father always says."

Tucked away in the cluster of giant trees was a small camper with an overhang. Nearby there was a firepit.

"This is where you come when you leave me?" she asked, taking it all in, processing the information.

"Every night," he said. "I've got a vision in my head of what it could be one day."

Skyler opened her arms, tilted her head back, spun around and breathed in the scent of the trees. They had a unique, sweet smell that was concentrated in that one area because of the density and age of the trees.

She stopped and opened her eyes; Hunter was watching her. "This is heaven on earth, Hunter."

Hunter ducked his head for a moment before he looked up with a sideways glance. "You think so?"

She leaned down to pick up an acorn, a large seed

from the oldest of the group, and put it in her pocket. "I know so. What a gift you will have to give to your wife one day. What an incredible, beautiful gift."

Chapter Five

That night, after he left Skyler at Liam's cabin, Hunter did something that he *never* did: he searched social media for images of Skyler. There was a guilty knot in his stomach; he wasn't exactly tied to Brandy McGregor and there hadn't been any promises made, but before the pandemic had changed everything about their lives, things were moving in a certain kind of direction with her. Their families approved of the match; in fact, both patriarchs thought it would be legacy building to have a marriage join the massive property holdings of the Brands and the McGregors. And if that marriage should produce a grandchild that could one day oversee a conglomeration of the two sets of property? Jock and Beau McGregor, Brandy's father, were salivating at the prospect. Still, Hunter had his doubts. If the pandemic hadn't happened, would he still be with Brandy? She was sweet and beautiful, yet a bit dull.

"There you are." Hunter had to create a new Instagram account, his first, in order to scroll through Skyler's history.

"Now who's the stalker?" he asked himself, enlarging a picture of Skyler before she had cancer. Before she lost her hair, it had been wispy and shoulder-length, a lovely golden, strawberry color that set off her lavender eyes in the most unusual way. With her hair just barely growing in, she reminded him of one of his mother's favorite actresses, Audrey Hepburn. Skyler had that same petite frame and sassy attitude. She was cute in the best sense of the word. Hunter imagined that it would be impossible, in general, to dislike Skyler. He'd certainly tried and failed rather quickly.

He was looking through Skyler's posted cancer journey when his best, and oldest, friend, Chase Rockwell, called.

"What's going on, man?" Chase asked him when he answered the phone.

"Just workin', what about you?"

"Same," his friend answered. Chase had inherited his family's farm and had been doing everything he could to keep it afloat. Chase had grown into one of the hardest-working men he'd ever known. Unfortunately, prior to his death, Chase's father had leveraged every piece of equipment on the farm and had taken out a second mortgage on the property.

"How's it going with the tourist?" Hunter hadn't had time to give his friend an update on Skyler.

"I don't really call her that," he said, feeling bad that he'd ever put that label out there.

"Huh. What *do* you call her?"

"Skyler."

"Give me her last name, man. I'm gonna look her up right now and see why you've done a one-eighty on this woman."

"Sinclair." Hunter didn't bother to play possum with his friend. Chase would just text someone in the family if he didn't give it to him. "I'm just going to send you a link to her Instagram page."

Hunter sent the information to his friend.

"Hold up. Since when are you on Instagram?"

"Since today."

Hunter didn't need to say anything more to Chase; the fact that he had broken his steadfast rule to avoid all things social media following the explosion of press, good and bad, after *Cowboy Up!* told his friend everything he needed to know. Skyler was different. His newfound interest in Skyler was different.

"She's cute. Not like your usual."

"No." He had always gone for tall, lanky, sun-kissed brunettes with rodeo and ranch credentials.

"Her friend Molly is...someone special..." Chase's voice trailed off and then after several seconds of silence, he said, "Ask Skyler to introduce us."

Hunter was floored. Chase hadn't shown much interest in dating since he'd lost Sarah. "You want to have a virtual date with a woman on the other side of the country?"

"Yeah. Why not? I can't do any worse than I'm doing here."

"Why not? I don't know. Maybe the fact that the two of you will most likely never be in the same place at the same time?"

"Maybe that will work in my favor," his friend joked. Then he added more seriously, "I'm tired of being alone. Everyone here knows my history. Everyone here knows about..." Chase stopped before he said her name. *Everyone knows about Sarah.*

There was some silence on the other end of the line while Chase moved through Skyler's social footprint.

"She had cancer?" His friend's voice had changed.

"Yeah, she did."

Chase let his breath out. "Man."

"I know," Hunter said. "I didn't get why Dad agreed to have a stranger come to the ranch especially during all of this COVID crap going on."

"Makes sense now."

"Yeah, it does."

"Sarah…" Chase said the name that was often spoken silently between them and thought of frequently, but rarely mentioned aloud.

"Sarah," Hunter echoed.

Sarah James had been the daughter of Jock's best friend. The story was that Hunter and Sarah were born a day apart, in the same hospital room, and they shared everything, including a playpen while their fathers played poker. As they grew up, Sarah became a second sister to him. He had never been able to see her as more than a sister, but all of his friends had crushes on her at one time or another. She was beautiful in an approachable, Jennifer Aniston kind of way—an athletic tomboy who felt just as comfortable in a cocktail dress, with a really loud, infectious laugh. But Sarah had only had eyes for Chase and the feeling was mutual.

"It's hard to believe that she's been gone ten years." Chase cleared his throat several times, and Hunter knew him well enough to know that he was fighting back emotion over a loss that was still raw for both of them.

During filming of the last season of *Cowboy Up!*, when Sarah made occasional appearances as Chase's girlfriend, she was diagnosed with a rare form of brain cancer called neuroblastoma. The cancer had been vicious, unrelenting and deadly. Hunter still felt the trauma of watching Sarah deteriorate so quickly and lose her battle with cancer in less than six months. They all did.

Jamie James, Sarah's father, whom everyone called J.J., took his daughter's death the hardest. He drank, he gambled and he got divorced. No one was surprised when J.J. had a catastrophic stroke and followed his daughter into the grave the following year. For Jock, the losses of J.J. and Sarah had been devastating; his father was a man cut from old-fashioned stock and didn't believe that men should ever cry. But Jock would get tears in his eyes at the mention of Sarah and he couldn't even say J.J.'s name without getting choked up.

"Man," Chase said again with a cough and a throat clear. "Heavy stuff."

"Yeah. I know. I'm sorry, Chase." Hunter wanted to redirect the conversation. "How are things going on your end? Did you get that tractor fixed?"

"Aw, I don't know, man." His friend sighed. "I think I'm gonna have to start selling off body parts. Do you know anyone in the market for a kidney?"

Everything hurt. Absolutely everything. Her inner thighs were sore, her butt cheeks were sore, her fingers were stiff from holding a pitchfork and her feet were dotted with blisters from breaking in her new boots. Skyler had taken to walking bow-legged inside of the cabin, hobbling about tenderly, groaning and saying "ouch" as she moved slowly from one room to the next.

"I thought this trip was supposed to make you feel better, not worse," Chester Sinclair said after his daughter ran down the list of ailments from working on the ranch.

"I feel better," she said with a laugh. "And worse."

Hunter had dug several splinters out of her hands before she finally remembered to put on her gloves when they tore down the remaining section of fence. She had also developed a heat rash under her arms that was itchy and burned all the time. At night she tucked washcloths with ice cubes wrapped inside under her arms for some relief. It seemed like she was a walking list of ailments, and yet she felt incredible mentally. She felt more powerful, more in control over her own destiny. She had torn down a fence with her bare hands!

"I'm getting stronger every day." She lifted up her arm and made a muscle for her father to see in the video chat. "Look. A baby muscle! When I got here, I couldn't lift a bale of hay. *Now* I can actually lift and carry it a couple of feet at a time. Just imagine how strong I'm going to be by the end of summer. You'll have to enter me in an iron-woman competition."

Chester smiled in spite of himself; even now, Skyler knew he wasn't convinced that Montana for the entire summer was the right choice.

"You could have done the same thing right here in the home gym with me," he countered, still smiling a bit.

"Anyway, I *am* excited for the family cookout," Skyler said, turning the conversation to a new topic.

"Well," Chester grumbled, "have fun. Be safe."

"I'll be safe. Don't worry."

"I always worry about you."

Skyler smiled. "And I love you for it."

"Have you ever driven a skid steer before?" Hunter smiled a bit at the way Skyler was walking—like an old, rickety cowboy.

"No."

"Well, hop on up. I'm going to show you right now."

The gravel for the main drive had been delivered, and between the two of them, the job was going to get done today.

"Okay," he said, once Skyler was seated in the skid steer and had the safety bar pulled down. "This is going to move just like the zero-turn lawn mower and the bucket is going to work like the bucket on the tractor. Basically, you know how to drive this thing already."

Skyler nodded; he had taught her how to tie a bandanna around her head so it would catch the sweat and stop if from dripping down into her eyes. Savannah had a spare hat, a dark brown Stetson that turned out to be a perfect fit for Skyler. Today, only two weeks after her arrival in Montana, Skyler looked like a different woman. She had put on some weight—good weight, the kind that came with building muscle. The grayish, pasty hue of her skin had been replaced by a golden, rosy glow. She had taken to wearing tank tops that defined her waist and showed off her slender, petite figure. Her jeans, roughed up and dirty from farm work, hugged her shapely bottom in a way that he found very sexy. In fact, he had to remind himself to focus on the work and not on how kissable he was finding her lips.

"See the green button overhead? Push that," he instructed. He was standing on the bucket of the skid steer, holding on to the safety handles, so close to her really that he could just lean forward and kiss her. It was mighty tempting but he knew it would be a stupid move. Jock would shoot him, stuff him and mount him over the fireplace if he screwed up with Skyler.

"Now turn the key."

Skyler started the skid steer and an elated smile lit up her face. Such a pretty face.

"Cool!" she exclaimed.

While he was standing on the bucket, Hunter had her practice both moving the skid steer forward and backward, and turning it from left to right.

"It's super easy," Skyler told him.

"Now, with your left foot, push your toe down to lift the bucket."

"With you on it?"

He nodded.

"I hope I don't fling you off," she said, biting her lip.

"You'll be fine," he reassured her. She carefully pressed down her left toe and jerked the bucket upward. Hunter held on to the handles tightly while he instructed her to lower the bucket by pressing down her left heel.

"It's counterintuitive," she observed.

"It takes some getting used to, but once you get it, it'll feel natural."

Hunter jumped off the bucket, then taught her how to pick up rock and then relocate it. It didn't take much practice before Skyler was barreling off in the skid steer, picking up gravel and dumping it in the washed-out areas of the long, main drive into Sugar Creek. With the tractor, he took a blade attachment and smoothed out the rock. They repeated this action time and again, working together, until all of the major potholes were filled in.

"My fingertips feel numb." Skyler hopped out of the skid steer after the job was done.

"It's from the vibration. It'll go away." He handed her a bottle of water.

She gulped down the water and then poured some of it on the back of her neck. There was dirt in the crease of her neck and dust covering both of her arms. Her tank top was soaked with sweat, her boots caked with dust and mud. In that moment, Skyler looked like a bona fide ranch woman and Hunter liked what he saw.

"I need one of these." Skyler patted the skid steer with her hand. "I don't know what the heck I would do with it in the city, or where I would park it. But I just really need one."

"You could always park it in the garage."

Skyler laughed. "I *live* in the garage. So *that* is not an option."

They climbed into his truck and he drove them back toward Liam's cabin.

"Look at this!" his companion said to him. "Look what we accomplished. This road isn't making me seasick anymore."

Her enthusiasm over the smallest of accomplishments on the ranch amused him. He'd never taken much pride in filling potholes with gravel—maybe he should start.

"I might've made it a bit worse on you than it needed to be," he admitted.

"I know." Skyler frowned at him playfully. "You wanted me gone in the worst way."

They rode in silence until they reached the turnoff toward the cabin. He slowed down so Skyler could enjoy the ride through the canopy of trees, something she had mentioned to him that she enjoyed.

"I don't feel that way anymore, you know." He didn't want her to think that he wanted her gone. He didn't.

Skyler glanced over at him with a shyness he wasn't used to seeing in her. "You don't?"

"No." He looked straight ahead through the windshield. "You've been a big help to me."

"Really?" She turned her body toward him…as much as the seat belt would allow. "Is that true?"

He nodded. It was true. That fence had been taken down a whole heck of a lot faster with her help, and filling in the potholes had gone quickly. Even when she had to take extended breaks, having her company made the jobs go by faster for him.

She seemed pleased with his confession. "Well, I'm glad. Because I'm having the time of my life."

Hunter dropped her off at the cabin with a promise to pick her up in two hours for the cookout; he watched her walk stiffly away from him. While he was watching, Skyler spotted a rock on the ground, bent down gingerly, picked it up, examined it and then put it in her pocket. She turned her head, caught him watching her, smiled and waved her hand, then continued her short journey to the cabin.

Hunter cranked the engine of the truck and then said to his phone, "Call Brandy."

"Call Brandy? Is that correct?"

"Yes."

"Okay. Calling Brandy."

As he turned the truck back to the main road, the phone rang twice and then Brandy picked up.

"Hey!" She sounded happy to hear from him. "I was just thinking about you."

Hunter drove under the canopy of trees and he looked up at the branches and the leaves. Being with Skyler had just made him more attentive to the beauty unfolding all around him on the ranch. Before her, he never would have bothered paying attention to the branches and leaves in the canopy.

"Then I guess it's a good thing I called," he said to Brandy. "Because I was just thinking about you, too."

"What do you think?" Skyler stepped in front of her phone camera so Molly could see the shift dress she had put on. "Too much?"

"This is just like a romantic-movie montage. You change into a bunch of different outfits and I shake my head and make a horrible face until we land on just the right outfit," her friend said, leaning forward to get a better look at the outfit.

"Except I've just tried on this one dress." Skyler looked down at the gauzy lavender dress with spaghetti straps and a thin belt to highlight her small waist.

"I was with you when you bought that," Molly said.

"I remember." She spun around, letting the skirt twirl around her legs. "What's the verdict?"

"I say yes," Molly responded. Her friend seemed distracted for a moment. Then she said, "You aren't going to believe this."

"What?"

Seemingly amazed, Molly looked up and said, "Chase just sent me a text."

"You said I could give him your number."

"I know, but..." Molly tucked some wayward curls behind her ear. "I guess I didn't really expect him to use it."

"I did. Hunter told me that Chase was really smitten with you."

"Did Chase actually use the word *smitten* or is that your word?"

"My word, I think." Skyler looked at her very short hair in the camera shot. "I wonder if I should wear my hat."

"He wants to know if he can call me later."

Skyler sat down on the bed and pulled on her socks. She had decided to wear her hat and her cowboy boots with the dress. It was a ranch cookout, after all.

"Say yes," she told Molly.

"I don't know." Her friend looked like she was frozen, but it wasn't a bad connection; she hadn't moved from her spot, seeming to be a bit stunned.

"You don't know?" Skyler frowned. "Why wouldn't you want to talk to him?"

"What if I don't like him? It will ruin countless hours of daydreaming from my youth. Those were wonderful daydreams. Do I really want the real him to ruin my fantasy of him?"

"Hunter says he's a real nice guy. Hardworking. Loyal. A great friend."

Molly fell backward on her bed and said dreamily, "Chase Rockwell."

Then her friend popped upright, a thoughtful expression on her pretty face. "It could be a double wedding, just like we always planned."

Skyler laughed at the thought. Hunter hadn't so much as looked at her with interest since she arrived. If anything, he treated her like an adored little sister. Much of her teenage fantasy of Hunter Brand of *Cowboy Up!* falling madly in love with her had given way to the reality of her relationship with him. Theirs was a budding friendship and she was happy with that. Would it have been nice to come to Montana and find a true romance with a cowboy? Of course. She was a true romance junkie—always had been, always would be. But her illness had taught her how to live in the moment, live for the day and live in reality.

"*Cowboy Up!* cowboys find love in the Big Apple?" Skyler teased her friend. "A sequel to the original series?"

"You never know." Molly refused to let her rain on her parade. "Stranger things have happened. I mean, seriously. A stranger thing just *did* happen!"

"Well, I think you should at least talk to him. It never hurts to have another friend in the world. Let me know what you decide. I love you," Skyler said and then waved goodbye. She went the extra mile and put on some mascara, a light dusting of blush and a clear gloss on her lips. She took some leather cleaner that Hunter had let her borrow and wiped down her boots before pulling them on. The multiple Band-Aids on her feet had made the boots more comfortable and allowed her to walk almost normally. Now if only the rash would go away and the soreness in her thighs and backside would subside.

She shut the front door behind her, still not used to the idea of leaving the door unlocked, and sat down. While she waited for Hunter, she checked her social media, thrilled to see how positive the responses were to all of her Montana posts. Hunter had been a reluctant photographer, but he had managed to capture great pictures of her working on the ranch. The latest picture of her driving the skid steer was her favorite to date. She looked strong. Happy. Capable.

Had she ever really looked that happy before in her life? The end of the summer was far off in the distance, but Skyler was already dreading the day that she had to leave Sugar Creek. How would she be able to go back to her small cubicle at the insurance company, sitting for hours day after day, answering complaints, when she knew that this life existed? How could she, really?

She heard the crunching of the tires of Hunter's truck as it approached. Skyler put away her phone and looked expectantly up the drive, awaiting the first glimpse of handsome Hunter behind the wheel of his truck. Every time she saw Hunter was like the first time—he still gave her the most wonderful butterflies in her stomach.

This wasn't a date. Of course it wasn't. But Skyler hoped that Hunter would like her in her dress. She stood up, put her hands on the porch rail and smiled in anticipation of seeing Hunter appear from beneath the canopy.

Hunter had taken particular care with his appearance for the cookout. He'd shaved his face, put on a clean button-down shirt and belt that displayed one of his most important trophies from his rodeo days—a large, intricately carved belt buckle. He donned a hat that wasn't covered in dirt and stains, and had almost put on cologne but decided against it.

"You look nice," Hunter said, enjoying the pretty sight of Skyler in her sundress as he approached her.

"Thank you." She gave him a twirl when she reached the bottom of the steps. "I didn't know if this was the right thing to wear."

"I think you did just fine," he said as he held out his arm for her. "May I escort you to the truck?"

She didn't hesitate to link her arm with his. "Why thank you, sir. So formal."

"That's how we do it in Montana." Hunter walked her to the passenger side of the truck. "A cookout is a big deal in these parts. I hope you're hungry," he added as he opened the truck door for her.

"Lately, all I can think about is eating."

"Then you're in luck. Because Mom and Aunt Lindsey have been cooking like they're feeding the entire town of Bozeman."

Hunter made sure she was safely in the truck, then shut the door, jogged to the other side and got behind the steering wheel.

"Do you want to take the trail to the main house or our new road?"

"The road that Hunter and Skyler built, of course," Skyler said and then she added seriously, "I really need to figure out how to get my hands on one of those skid steers."

Chapter Six

"I know why you were so insistent about opening the ranch to Skyler," Hunter said to his father.

Jock wasn't a tall man, but he was broad-shouldered and barrel-chested, and held himself with the presence of a man who had scraped and clawed his way to the top of the heap. He had a bright, thick head of white hair brushed straight back from his weathered, deeply lined face. His hawkish nose was a prominent feature of his face, as were his snapping, keenly intelligent ocean-blue eyes.

Hunter hadn't said Sarah's name out loud, but he saw Jock turn his head away and swallow several times, hard, before he said anything else.

"Well, she seems to be a nice young lady," Jock

said of Skyler, who was down by the pond with Bruce, Savannah, Amanda and their pack of rescue dogs. Jock completely avoided the subject of Sarah and Hunter decided it was best to move on.

"Yes, she is," Hunter agreed.

Skyler had managed to endear herself to the family without much effort at all. Perhaps it was her pixie-like appearance, or her bright, easy laugh. Perhaps it was how kind and thoughtful she was to everyone around, including, or perhaps especially, the children in the bunch.

"Anything else to report?"

"No." Hunter crossed his arms casually in front of his body. "We've been taking it real slow."

"Good to hear."

"She's a hard worker. A real hard worker."

Jock looked at him sideways with his keen, appraising eyes. "So you've said."

"But she just doesn't have the stamina for this life."

"It takes time," his father noted. "Especially after what she's been through."

"Maybe." Hunter wasn't convinced. Skyler always gave her best effort and never gave up, but he didn't think she was built for Montana life. Not long-term, anyway.

There was a short silence between them before his father asked, "Have you spoken to Brandy McGregor lately?"

"Today," he said, not wanting to go down that road with his father. After speaking with Brandy, Hunter couldn't stop thinking about the fact that he had everything in common with Brandy and very little to say to her. In sharp contrast, at least in his mind, was the fact that he always had something he wanted to share with Skyler. Even after he had spent the day with her, he would go home and think of something he should share with Skyler the next day.

"Your mother and I both hope things are still heading in the right direction in that regard. I know Brandy's father is of a like mind."

"I'm well aware of everyone's feelings."

Hunter could see Jock getting all revved up to harp some more on the subject when his mother, Lilly, thankfully interrupted him.

"Do you think that Skyler would enjoy a pair of moccasins?" His mother held a pair of moccasins in her hands.

His mother was a proud member of the Chippewa Cree tribe and she had learned how to make authentic native clothing when she was a young girl growing up on the Rocky Boy's Indian Reservation.

"I think she would be really honored to receive those, Momo."

A beautiful woman with long, straight silver-laced raven hair, his mother was a gentle spirit who always managed to temper Jock's gruff, demanding ways. Lilly smiled and tucked the moccasins under her arm. "I will wrap them up for later."

Lilly called the family together to take a seat at the picnic tables set away from each other so each family group could safely join the event. Each picnic table had bowls and platters with the evening's fare. It was odd to eat separately from his family; everyone usually sat together in their family group. They were used to gathering every Sunday morning in the dining room in the main house.

"Look at all of this food!" Skyler slipped off her mask and sat down next to him at the table. "This is a feast!"

Hunter enjoyed watching his dinner companion load her plate like she hadn't eaten for months. She piled up mashed potatoes, corn on the cob with a pat of butter, green beans and ribs on her plate, then topped it off with a dinner roll.

"You can have seconds, you know," he said before he took a big bite out of one of his mother's famous homemade butter rolls.

Skyler nodded her response, too busy digging in to the mashed potatoes and gravy. "Mmm. Homemade mashed potatoes."

"Homemade everything," Hunter corrected.

"Lucky." Skyler loaded her fork with green beans. "I was raised almost exclusively on Chinese takeout. My mom, God love her, couldn't boil water."

Hunter noted that Skyler spoke of her mother in

the past tense, but didn't want to broach a subject that could ruin the fun she was having devouring his mom's home-cooked food.

"Your family is really great," she said, in between large gulps of Savannah's fresh-squeezed lemonade. "I think I met almost all of your brothers. And their wives. And their kids. And their dogs."

Skyler did have seconds; he didn't know where she managed to put all of that food away.

"I'm stuffed," she said a while later, and put her hands on her belly, which was slightly rounded now from all the food she had eaten. "I can't remember ever eating so much. But everything was just so good."

"It's the ranch work. You're burning calories," Hunter told her. "Mom will pack up some doggy bags for you, if you want."

She wiped her mouth with a napkin. "I absolutely want. That will be my midnight snack, breakfast, lunch and dinner tomorrow."

"Mom is going to be very pleased that you enjoyed her cooking."

Skyler leaned her elbows on the table now that they were done eating. Her eyes took in the expansive landscape before them. Beyond the pond were cows grazing in the long grass, and beyond that view was the mountain range off in the distance. Skyler sighed beside him.

"What's on your mind?"

"Nothing, really," she said quietly. "Everything."

She breathed in deeply and then let out the breath with another sigh. "I'm here. With you and your family. At Sugar Creek Ranch. It's an incredible privilege. This same time last year, I didn't think I would be alive, much less sitting here in Montana with you and your family. I'll never understand why Jock agreed to this, but I will be forever grateful."

Hunter had thought about telling Skyler about Sarah…and maybe one day he would. But for now, he just couldn't bring himself to talk about his loss with someone who hadn't known her. It was painful enough broaching the subject with Chase.

"I'm sure he had his reasons." That was all Hunter could think to say in response.

As the sun set, the family began to clean up the cookout and return to their homes. Skyler insisted on helping Lilly take all of the bowls and dishes into the kitchen, which was just off the back patio. It was the smaller of two kitchens in the main house and the one that Lilly often used to cook for outdoor family events.

"Thank you so much for inviting me," Skyler said to Jock and Lilly. "Thank you for everything, really."

"We are so happy to have you here with us," Lilly said sincerely. "I think it will be a healing summer for my son and for you."

Skyler glanced over at him curiously. Wanting to move past the moment and not have Skyler ask his mother questions about her statement, Hunter asked, "Don't you have something you wanted to give Skyler, Mom?"

Lilly's eyes lit up. "Oh, yes! Wait right here."

Lilly walked quickly back to the kitchen.

"You've been enjoying yourself?" Jock asked Skyler in his gruff, scratchy voice.

"I have."

"Good. Good." His father nodded.

That was followed by an awkward silence between the three of them until Lilly reappeared with a small box that she had managed to find time to wrap with tissue paper.

"A welcome gift." Lilly held out the box.

"Thank you so much, Mrs. Brand." Skyler accepted the box. "Should I open it now?"

"If you'd like." His mother nodded.

Skyler took the box to a nearby table, and carefully, slowly, unwrapped the paper from the box. It occurred to Hunter that Skyler must take hours to unwrap her presents at Christmastime. After the wrapping paper was carefully removed, and Skyler had folded it neatly next to the box, she lifted the lid and peeked inside.

Joy. That was the expression on Skyler's face when she saw the moccasins. "Oh, Mrs. Brand. They are beautiful."

"She made those," Hunter told Skyler, sure that she didn't realize that they had been designed, constructed and decorated with intricate beadwork by his mother's hands.

Skyler lifted one moccasin out of the box and examined the flower pattern embellishment on the toe.

"You made these?"

"It's a hobby." Lilly had always been humble about her talent, which Hunter always appreciated about her.

"Well… I hate to break up the party, but I'm going to bed," Jock said abruptly. "Young lady—you let me know if Hunter gives you any trouble."

"He's been great to me," Skyler said quickly, and if Hunter was detecting it correctly, a little defensively.

"Good night." His father waved his hand like he was swatting at a fly before he headed back to the house.

"Thank you, again, Mrs. Brand."

"Please, call me Lilly."

Hunter saw how his mother and Skyler were looking at each other—there was a genuine connection there. A mutual affection had grown quickly.

Skyler folded the moccasin carefully into the box and the put the lid back on. She seemed emotional when she said to his mom, "Lilly, I will cherish these for the rest of my life."

A week after the cookout, some of Skyler's aches and pains had subsided and she was regularly getting up in the morning before daybreak without any help from Hunter. In fact, she was usually just finishing up with the barn chores when he pulled in to pick her up for whatever list of jobs he had it in mind to complete that day. There was plenty to love about ranch life and some of it had actually lived up to her teenage fantasies. But the reality of the life was difficult for Skyler to imagine day in, day out for the rest of her life. She missed takeout and Starbucks and Bloomingdale's. She missed her friends and hanging at her father's garage.

Skyler let Zodiac and Dream Catcher out in the paddock after their morning grain and then she quickly mucked the stalls. In the beginning, she couldn't do the barn by herself, and now she could. This was a source of pride for her; she was getting stronger every day. Of course, her dad was right— she could have done the same thing in a gym. She wouldn't have done it, though—that's the truth. She hated lifting weights and riding on a stationary bike. No thank you! But lifting a fifty-pound bale of hay was doing the same thing for her as lifting weights, maybe even more.

Skyler was filling the freshly scrubbed water buckets with water to get ahead of the evening barn chores when she heard the tiniest of meows. She turned off the water and looked around.

"Hey, there." She saw a dainty gray tabby with

four white sock feet and a perky, long tail sitting just outside of the barn.

The tabby had pretty green eyes and it made eye contact with her, then meowed again as if to say "hi." Skyler put down the water hose and squatted in the center aisle.

"Come here, sweet thing." She tried to coax the kitty into the barn.

Once the cat realized that she was a friend, it stood up, stretched and walked toward her, its long tail straight up in the air.

"I like to see that you are proud to be you," Skyler said. "You walk with your tail straight up in the air. Good for you!"

The kitty cat walked right over to where she was squatting, trilled sweetly and then rubbed up against her several times. Skyler reached out her hand to let the feline sniff her fingers.

"Where did you come from?" she asked the loving creature. "You don't have a collar or a tag."

The kitty cat trilled again, threw itself down on the ground, rolled, stretched and began to purr loudly. The cat gazed at Skyler with loving eyes and curled its paws in a show of feline affection.

"You are too sweet, aren't you?" Skyler stood up. "I wonder if you're hungry? You look a little skinny."

She walked outside of the barn toward the cabin, and when she glanced behind her, the cat was following her, hugging the shrubbery and trotting to keep up.

"Okay," Skyler told the kitty. "You stay here and I will get you something to eat."

Inside the cabin, Skyler rummaged in the fridge, grabbing some leftover chicken, a plate and a bowl for water. She finished her chore quickly because she was afraid that the cat would leave if she was gone for too long.

"Oh, good!" Skyler exclaimed when she saw the gray tabby sitting on the porch. "I found something superdelicious for you."

The moment she put the chicken down, the cat began to devour it in a way that let Skyler know that it had missed some meals. Next to the plate, Skyler put down the bowl of water.

The cat seemed to think that Skyler was going to leave and she moved away from the bowl, anxiously following her and leaving the food.

"I'm just going to sit right here next to you," Skyler explained, sitting down on the top step of the porch stairs. "You eat. I'm not going anywhere."

The kitty ate several bites, then came over to rub up against Skyler for a few moments, then went back to the food. The cat executed this ritual several times until the chicken was gone. After it had cleaned the plate, the cat gratefully climbed into Skyler's lap and began to purr loudly and contentedly, while gazing up at her with love in its eyes.

"You're welcome." Skyler smiled down at the cat. "I love you, too.

Skyler was still holding the cat as it fell asleep in her lap when Hunter pulled up.

"I have a new friend," she said to the cowboy.

"That's one of the rescue cats from the main barn," Hunter said. "She's not the strongest mouser, I can tell you that. I don't think she's caught one since we've had her."

"She was starving, I think."

"May be why she found her way down here," Hunter told her. "I've seen her try to catch all kinds of insects without any success at all."

"Does she have a name?" Skyler rubbed the top of the purring cat's head.

"I think Amanda called her Rosy at one time."

"I don't really like that name."

"Well, she seems to be yours now," Hunter said. "Name her what you want."

Skyler looked down at the slender, small-boned cat and an image of her mother's favorite flower popped into her head. "Daisy. I think your name is Daisy."

The cat held the eye contact, blinked slowly as a means of communicating love and then meowed.

Skyler laughed and said to Hunter, "She just agreed with the name."

"Okay." The cowboy's eyebrows drew down a bit as he checked his phone. "Are you ready to go?"

"Yep." Skyler gently displaced Daisy. "Now, you stay nearby. I'll be back later."

To Hunter she said, "I need to go into town to get some cat food today."

He nodded. As they walked toward the truck, he asked, "Why Daisy?"

"It was my mom's favorite flower."

"It's just you and your dad now?"

Skyler opened the door to the truck and climbed into what she had begun to think of her spot in the copilot's chair. "My mom passed away when I was nineteen."

"Well, I'm real sorry to hear that," Hunter said.

"Thank you."

As Hunter drove them slowly through her favorite canopy of trees, she asked, "What are we doing today?"

"Worming cattle."

Hunter had been taking it easy on Skyler and he'd put some things on the back burner, but some chores couldn't be delayed and the biannual worming of the cattle was one of those chores. Hunter drove them to a large barn that serviced a smaller herd near the southern property line of the ranch.

"I love the calves with the white faces," Skyler said. "They are too cute."

"I'm not a fan."

"Why not?"

"Those babies belong to the cleanup bull. Which means we wasted a heck of a lot of money and time."

"What's a cleanup bull?"

They met each other in front of the truck. "You see, we bought some top-notch semen—"

"Bought it."

"Yes. We bought semen from what we rated as superior bulls and used that semen to artificially inseminate the females who are in heat."

"How do you do that?"

Hunter squinted at her. "You really want to know that?"

"Sure. Why not?"

"Well, you put them in a chute mainly, put on a plastic protective glove that goes up to your bicep, lift up the cow's tail, stick your hand into the canal… Heck, my arm will go in up past my elbow. Then you slide in this long rod that allows you to inject the semen and then the deed is pretty much done."

"You do that?"

"I have one of the best records in the state for using AI. But just in case the insemination process doesn't work, we use a cleanup bull to come behind us and try to get it done the old-fashioned way," Hunter explained.

"I see."

"I do, too." Hunter nodded toward the babies. "A bunch of offspring of the cleanup bull."

That made Skyler laugh, and her face lit up with

humor. "All the white-faced babies belong to the cleanup bull?"

"Every last one of 'em."

"He did such a good job."

Hunter frowned at what he could only see as a giant waste of money and time. "He brought my batting average way down."

Hunter walked to the back of the truck, pulled some premixed wormer solutions in metal spray bottles out of the bed and headed toward the corral. Skyler tagged along after him.

"Now, you've got to watch yourself in the pen with the cows. Even the babies can accidentally knock you over. They wouldn't mean to do it—they're docile creatures, but they are strong and heavy."

"I'll be careful."

"See that you are," he said sternly. "You could get killed."

Skyler saluted Hunter behind his back and followed him into the holding pen, where a small group of cows and their babies were held. The smell of cow urine and manure was so strong that it made her gag a little bit. When she stepped inside the pen, her boots sank into the mud and manure, squishing as she walked, and made a sucking noise when she lifted her foot, one at a time, out of the muck.

Carefully, she picked her way through the cows, smiling at them and talking gently to them. The babies were often curious, coming up to her and trying to nudge her.

"Hi, sweet baby." Skyler petted one of the cleanup bull's babies. "Aren't you cute?"

"We are going to herd them into this round pen and then, one by one, spray this solution on their backs, along their spines. This will help with worms and lice."

"Lice?" Skyler withdrew her hand quickly from the calf.

Hunter ignored her, focused entirely on moving the cows into the round pen. He waved his arms and walked slowly toward them, herding them into the adjacent pen. Skyler joined him, waving her arms and herding the cows.

"They all need a bath." Skyler's face was wrinkled up from trying to avoid the smell. "Why are they all so dirty?"

"They're cows. They live outside. They get dirty."

"Ugh." She made an effort to only breathe through her mouth. "I like them very much, but they are stinky."

"It's the cow manure. It's got its own particular aroma."

"Aroma?" she asked. "That's an awfully fancy term for what I'm smelling right now."

Once they got the cows into the round pen, Hunter handed her a heavy metal spray can. "I'll get the first in line and you get the second. We'll get this done double time."

Skyler had her mouth hanging open to avoid the smell and managed to suck a fly into her mouth. She squinted her eyes and spat out the fly, then continued spitting until she was convinced that all of the residual fly germs were out of her mouth. She stood upright, looked over at Hunter, who was waiting for her to get to work, and said, "I'm ready now."

The job went quickly and, although hot and stinky, it wasn't terribly difficult. Her arm did ache from using the same spraying motion again and again and her fingers hurt from holding on to the metal spray canister. But, all in all, she was pleased with her work.

"Now what?" she asked once the last cow was treated.

"We'll let them out in the pasture."

Skyler wove her way through the mooing, slow-moving cows, and encountered a calf, the smallest of the cleanup bull's offspring.

"You know," she said, "you might be a little stinky, but I still love you."

The calf rubbed against her and nuzzled her hand. Skyler bent down to hug the calf. Then something startled the calf, perhaps the sound of Hunter opening the gate, but it bolted to the side and Skyler fell backward with a loud thud and a definitive splat.

Chapter Seven

"Uh!" Her entire backside was covered in the manure-mud mixture. Her arms, her hands, the back of her head, her neck, the back of her pants and shirt—Skyler's whole body was covered with the slimy, stinky concoction. Her hat had fallen off her head and had been pressed into the mud by the calf.

"Oh, no." Skyler pushed herself up to a standing position, her entire hand immersed in the muck. "Oh."

"Are you all right?" Hunter had seen her fall and rushed to her side.

"Am I all right?" she snapped, holding her arms and hands out from her body like she was a scarecrow. "No! I'm not all right. Look at me!"

A family of flies were buzzing around her, trying to land on her clothing and her hair. "Get away from me, flies!"

Skyler swung her arms in the air, trying to dissuade the annoying insects from landing on her. She didn't know what to do; she was a mess. A stinky, terrible mess.

"What am I going to do? How am I going to get home?" She raised her voice, squishing her way to the gate that would take her out of the paddock. "I can't get in your truck like this."

"No," Hunter said with a smirk on his face.

"Quit laughing at me!" she snapped, waving her arms to move the flies away from her.

"I'm not laughing."

"Yes, you are." She complained, "I'm covered in manure and you're laughing at me instead of helping me."

"Okay," the cowboy said, trying to look serious. "We have a couple of choices."

"Which are?" She narrowed her eyes at him impatiently.

"First, you could just ride in the back of the truck and we'll get you home that way."

"Option one, I stay covered in manure and ride in the back of your truck. I can't wait to hear option two."

"We hose you off."

"Hose me off?"

"It's an option."

Skyler couldn't stand the thought of spending one more second in her current condition. "Fine. Where's the hose?"

As they walked together back toward the barn, Hunter, she noticed, kept a safe distance from her.

"I should hug you right now," she said, swerving toward him.

Hunter laughed and tacked to the right, away from her. "I did tell you to be careful. What were you doing?"

"Hugging one of the cleanup bull's calves."

Hunter turned on the hose and let the hot water run out.

"Wash my hands and arms first. Please." Skyler held out her hands, wanting to get them clean ASAP.

The cowboy followed her directive and washed off her hands and arms first before he began the chore of rinsing off her neck and back.

"That's cold," Skyler complained again, jumping around as the frigid water hit her skin and soaked her clothing.

"I don't remember telling you to hug the calves."

"You didn't say *not* to hug them." Skyler scowled at him.

"I kind of thought that might be a given," he said, his voice laced with humor at her expense. "Cover your face with your hands so I can get the back of your head."

When he was done with his chore, her clothes were completely soaked and water dripped from her onto the ground.

"I'm soaking wet!"

"That's the physics of water," he said seriously, but she could see a pleased smirk lingering on his face.

"I can't get into your truck like this." She bemoaned her current state of being. Now she was wet and squishy; the material of her jeans was sticking to her skin, and she felt cold and clammy.

"No."

She stared up at him. "You want me to ride in the back of your truck, don't you?"

He rubbed his chin thoughtfully. "Would you mind? I just had the inside cleaned."

"I'm soaking wet here!" When she waved her arms, droplets of water flew out around her.

"I think I have a towel in the truck," he said, as if he'd just remembered.

She followed behind him, her wet socks slushing inside her boots. He fished a towel out of one of the large toolboxes in the bed of his truck.

She took it gratefully, wiping off her hands, arms and face first. She rubbed the towel over her short hair then she tried to sop up some of the water that was in her tank top and jeans.

"I still reek like cow manure." She sniffed herself.

"Yes, you do," he agreed, too readily for her liking.

"And I'm wet."

"Yes, you are."

After a second or two of thought, she said, "Take off your shirt."

"Excuse me?"

"Don't act scandalized, Hunter. You heard me. Take off your shirt and then turn around. I'm getting out of these clothes."

Hunter's lips quirked up into a half smile and his electric blue eyes sparkled with humor. She could only imagine the things he wanted to say, the sexual innuendos just dying to get out. But, to his credit, he kept them to himself.

Hunter tugged his shirttail loose from his jeans and began to unbutton his shirt. The first couple of buttons exposed the smooth skin of his chest, which was a couple of shades lighter than the skin at his neck, and then the next buttons revealed the top of his six-pack abs. *The man must do sit-ups in his spare time or something*, she thought to herself before she realized, too late, that she was blatantly staring at him while he undressed.

Hunter shrugged out of his plaid button-down shirt, then offered it to her and slowly took his own sweet time turning around.

"Thank you." She took the shirt and then scurried behind the truck.

"Oh, this feels terrible." She pulled off her tank

top and bra, watching Hunter to make sure he didn't turn around and catch her in the buff.

She quickly slipped on his shirt, noticing that the shirt held Hunter's woodsy, salty scent. It was a smell that made her senses tingle in the nicest of ways. Next, she pulled off her boots and stood in her socks while she fought to push her wet jeans over her hips and thighs.

"Come on!" she grunted, tugging and pushing and struggling until she was finally able to yank off the jeans.

Her underwear was damp but not completely wet or ruined by the manure. She left them on and tied the towel around her waist like a bathing-suit wrap. Leaving her socks on, she scooped up her dirty clothes and tossed them into the bed of the truck.

"Okay," she said, coming around the side of the truck. "You can turn around now."

Hunter turned around, swept his eyes up and down her body in a way that made her believe that he was looking at her, maybe for the first time, like a woman, and not like his little sister. He smiled at her.

"You look good in my shirt."

She had to be blushing; no doubt about it. "My hat is ruined."

Hunter opened the door to his truck so she could climb in. "Don't worry about it. We'll get you a new one."

* * *

"Hunter!" A silky female voice saying his name caught his attention. "I was just talking about you."

Hunter turned around to see Brandy McGregor walking through the doors of the Four Corners Saddlery tack shop.

Brandy, her shiny brunette hair worn long and loose, framing her stunning face, made a beeline for him. She wasn't wearing a mask.

"This is a real treat. All we've had since I've gotten back were phone calls and video dates." His pretty neighbor pouted her full lips, drawing attention to them deliberately, he was sure.

Brandy threw her arms around him affectionately and hugged him tightly. "You know, Dustin has been asking me out but I told him that you had already beat him to the front of the line."

"I've been real busy." Hunter adjusted the bandanna over his mouth. He could see Skyler watching them out of the corner of his eye.

"I know." Brandy made a frustrated noise. "It's not your fault Jock's making you babysit this summer." She reached out and tugged playfully on his sleeve. "Why don't you make an excuse—tell Jock that we need your help over at Boulder Ridge and we can sneak off and have ourselves a little fun."

"What do you think of this one?" Skyler asked, modeling a hat.

Brandy's brow furrowed as her attention turned to where Skyler was standing. "Is that...?"

"That's our guest."

"Oh," his neighbor drawled. "You're calling her a *guest* now. I think I'll go over and introduce myself."

Crap.

Hunter followed Brandy over to where Skyler was trying on hats to replace the one trampled by the cleanup bull's offspring.

"Hiya." Brandy sauntered over to Skyler with her long-legged, stride. "I'm Brandy."

"Skyler."

It was a small space and even though Skyler had her mask on, Hunter was glad that she moved a step or two away from Brandy.

"I like that one," Brandy said of the hat Skyler was trying on.

"Really?" Skyler looked at her own appearance. "I wasn't sure."

"You just have to sit it back on your head a bit." Brandy pointed to her own hat.

Skyler studied her reflection and for the briefest of moments caught his gaze in the mirror. He gave her a thumbs-up.

It was a good color for her; the deep walnut-brown offset her wide lavender eyes.

"You look as adorable as a bug," Brandy gushed. "Doesn't she, Hunter?"

"It looks good on her." He agreed, eager to buy the hat and go.

"Are you enjoying your time at Sugar Creek?" Brandy asked Skyler. "Hunter has just told me oodles and oodles about you. I was hoping I'd get a chance to meet you."

"I'm enjoying it," Skyler said and Hunter noted how toned-down her response was. Usually, Skyler was over the moon about her time in Montana and she wasn't typically afraid to express it.

"Well, I'm so glad you're enjoying your little summer vacation with us." Brandy rested her arm on his sleeve and Hunter saw Skyler's eyes dart to the hand and then back up to Brandy's face.

"It was very nice to meet you, Brandy," Skyler said after she paid for her hat. "Thank you for the hat advice," she said as she exited.

"Of course. It was my pleasure," Brandy called out as she hooked her arm with Hunter's. "Don't keep me waiting too long," she said, lowering her voice for his ears only. "I'm getting awfully lonesome. Daddy doesn't like to see me lonesome."

Hunter extracted himself from Brandy as diplomatically as he could and then he hurried out of the store, where he found Skyler waiting for him at the truck.

Something subtle in Skyler's body language signaled to him that she felt upset or uncomfortable. How did he know this about her? He just did.

"Don't forget we need to get cat food for Daisy," Skyler said in a subdued tone. She buckled herself into the seat and looked straight ahead, her new hat in her lap.

Hunter drove her to the nearest grocery store and wished that Skyler wouldn't be so quiet. He was used to her chatting his ear off, something he had thought he didn't like. Now that it was gone, he wanted it back. After a quick trip in and out of the grocery store, Hunter asked, "Anywhere else?"

"I want to go home," she said, staring out the passenger window.

"I hope you mean just back to the cabin."

It felt like a sharp, hot poker had stabbed him in the gut when he thought that Skyler might be saying that she wanted to go home to New York. When she didn't clarify her statement, Hunter decided it was best to just leave her to her thoughts. He switched on the radio and turned the music down low.

Every now and again he would look over at Skyler, wishing he knew how to break her out of her current mood. Yes, Brandy had laid it on thick back at the store; no doubt her sugary sweet tone had come off as anything but sweet to Skyler. Brandy had acted like a territorial huntress with Skyler, and he, not knowing *what* to do, like an idiot, had done *nothing*. When they pulled onto the Sugar Creek main drive, his companion still hadn't said a word to him. As he always did, he drove slowly through

Skyler's favorite tree canopy, half expecting her to break the silence and point out to him, for the one hundredth time, that the sun filtering through the branches and leaves looked like fireworks in a forest-green sky. But she said nothing.

"We're home," he said, shifting into Park.

Skyler pushed the door open a bit harder than normal and jumped out of the truck. "This isn't my home, Hunter. You know it and I know it."

Skyler slammed the truck door and marched, a little tenderly still, as indignantly as she could toward the cabin.

"Damn it." Hunter held on to the steering wheel until his knuckles turned white.

Instead of doing what he knew he *should* do, he did what he *wanted* to do: he followed Skyler. He hopped out of his truck and jogged after her.

"She's not my girlfriend," he called after her.

"I didn't ask."

"But you care."

Skyler spun around and pointed her finger at him. "Don't tell me how I feel, Hunter. You don't know how I feel."

"Then why don't you tell me?"

"I hate women like that! All of that talking-out-of-both-sides-of-your-mouth, sugary-sweet, mean-girl, butter-won't-melt-in-my-mouth crap! I know that I'm short and skinny and my hair is a weird shade of red. I know I don't have big boobs or any boobs to speak of. I always have to fight against my own negative newsreel! I don't need some random stranger to deliberately try to make me feel bad about myself for no other reason than she's an overly possessive, insecure, jealous wench! If she *is* your girlfriend, you've got real questionable taste!"

"She's not my girlfriend. Not really."

Skyler breathed in deeply and bit her lip hard while she shook her head and looked up at the sky for a moment.

"'Not really' is not a status, Hunter."

"You've never asked me if I have a girlfriend."

"That's right," Skyler snapped. "And you've never asked me if I have a boyfriend."

"Do you have a boyfriend?"

Daisy appeared and trotted up the stairs, where Skyler greeted her gently and kindly. Skyler pulled the cat food out of the grocery bag and tried to rip it open. She tried several times before Hunter walked up the stairs, took the bag from her, opened it and then poured Daisy some food.

"The answer is *no*. I don't have a boyfriend." Skyler crossed her arms in front of her body. "Jeremy couldn't handle my illness so we both thought it was for the best if we broke up. So we did. End of story.

"I have to go take care of the horses now," she said, brushing by him and racing down the steps.

"I'll help you."

"I don't need your help." Skyler picked up the pace.

"Will you just stop, Skyler?" Hunter called after her, frustrated. "You're acting like a teenager."

That got her to stop. She spun around, pointed to her chest and said, "I'm not acting like a teenager. I'm acting *hurt*. I was having a great time with you and then a frickin' Victoria's Secret model, your *girlfriend*, insulted me by calling me a cute bug."

"Adorable," Hunter mumbled.

"What?"

"I think she said adorable."

"Do you want to see adorable?" Skyler asked, holding up her middle finger. "Here's adorable for you."

"Hold up." Hunter picked up his pace; he reached for her hand and caught it, but let it go when she pulled away.

"I don't even know why I feel so mad at you right now." She turned to face him.

"Because you care."

He could see the hurt in her eyes and he was sorry for it. The wires had just gotten crossed between them. They had been developing a friendship—a working relationship—and somewhere along the line, something else had developed between them. He felt it, and now he was certain that she was feeling it, too.

"What if I do?" she asked with a shrug.

He took a step toward her, holding the eye contact. "What if *I* do?"

Disbelief—that was what he read in her large lavender eyes.

"I'm sorry about what happened with Brandy—I didn't know how to react so I did nothing. I was an idiot."

Silence was her response.

"But she isn't my girlfriend. She's home from graduate school because of the pandemic and we've been talking. That's it."

"That's a lot."

"Not to me," Hunter said, exasperated. "I'm much more interested in what's going on right here. Right now. Between us."

"The horses are waiting."

"Let them wait." Hunter had a demanding tone in his voice.

Skyler's arms were crossed in front of her body, but she didn't leave the conversation.

Hunter dipped his head down, lowered and softened his voice.

"I feel a certain way about you, Skyler."

She didn't move; she didn't say a word. She listened, keenly, to what he was saying.

"I don't know exactly what this is, but I want to figure it out." He hooked his fingers with hers; he wanted to test the waters. Would she accept this physical touch from him?

Instead of pulling away, she actively held on to his fingers.

As he held her fingers, he held her gaze.

"I feel connected to you, Skyler." The words were coming out more from his heart than his head. "Connected in a way that doesn't make sense to me, in a way that I've never quite felt before. If you don't feel the same way about me, then tell me now and I'll get one of my brothers to take over for me..."

Skyler's breath caught as she took a sharp intake of oxygen. He didn't need her to say the words; the raw emotion he read in her eyes was enough for him.

Hunter acted on the feeling and kissed her. Still holding on to her hand, he pressed his lips to hers, being gentler and more patient than he had ever been before.

Her lips were soft and the kisses hesitant, but so very sweet.

Hunter took her face in his hands. "You are so beautiful, Skyler."

He read the rejection of that compliment in her eyes.

"You are." He dropped butterfly kisses on her lips. "My lovely, unusual, magical, unexpected angel."

Chapter Eight

Skyler's moral compass was temporarily rendered out of order by the fact that Hunter Brand was kissing her and declaring that he had feelings for her. It was a scene that could be taken out of hundreds of her teenage daydreams. But then reality set it and her moral compass lurched back to center.

"That was a lousy thing to do." She pushed on his chest and took a step back from him. "Brandy is waiting for your call, remember? You're playing both sides against the middle, Hunter. No woman deserves that."

"Is that what this is all about?" Hunter asked, frustrated. "The fact that I've been talking to Brandy?"

Skyler didn't respond; she turned on her heel and headed toward the barn.

"I'll take care of this right now," Hunter said.

She turned around. "What are you doing?"

He held up his hand to stop her from interrupting him while he held the phone up to his ear.

"Hey," he said after the call connected. "Yeah, it's always good to see you, too, Brandy."

Skyler crossed her arms in front of her body; Hunter had actually called Brandy.

"Look," he said, "if you want to go out with Dustin, don't say no on account of me. I think we're better off as friends."

Hunter glanced up at her while he listened to Brandy on the other end of the line. He nodded wordlessly and then he said, "I understand. You take care."

The cowboy put away his phone and walked over to her with long-legged strides. In truth, she didn't know how to react—she didn't know what to do, so she did nothing. She stood her ground and waited.

"That's done," he said dispassionately.

"Just like that." It was both a statement and a question.

"Just like that."

"And how did Brandy feel about—" she snapped her fingers "—'just like that'?"

"She thinks I'm a jackass and she told me not to call her anymore."

"Huh," Skyler said.

Hunter breathed in deeply and let it out with a frustrated noise. "Brandy collects cowboys like a sport. I'm no more important to her than she is to me.

"Now..." he said, dipping his head down, his eyes scanning her face with an appreciation that she couldn't ignore. This man—this cowboy of her dreams—returned her interest, her attraction. "Can we focus on what is going on, right here, right now, between us?"

It had been completely unexpected, Hunter's declaration of feelings. He had always been polite, solicitous and teasing, but only once, when she had donned his shirt, had she ever sensed that he saw her as an attractive woman.

The kiss. Her mind was always returning to that wonderful, romantic, tender kiss. She had always imagined how his lips would feel if he pressed them against hers. Now she didn't have to wonder. Because it had actually happened. So new was this development between Hunter and her that she hadn't even shared it with Molly. In all the years they had been friends, this was the first time that she had wanted to keep something just for herself. She would, of course, tell Molly—she would tell Molly before she told anyone else. For now, she wanted to savor it, to make it last. She worried, with a tinge of superstition that she had always possessed, that to speak about it aloud would be to risk making it disappear.

"I've got the horses saddled for us." Hunter walked up to where she was sitting on the porch steps with Daisy.

It was nighttime and the moon was full, washing the treetops with a buttery yellow hue. While they spent the day working together, there was no mention of the kiss the day before; there was no mention of the feelings Hunter had confessed he had for her. They kidded and joked and teased, but they kept it light, which suited Skyler just fine. Cancer had focused her mind singularly on the present, but she was very much aware of the future. At best, this would be a summer romance with Hunter. She had a real life back home; it was a smaller, more compact, more mundane life in the city. But it was hers. And there was her dad to think about. Without her, he would be alone. She *was* his family. Unlike Hunter, she didn't have multiple siblings and an extended family in the state. For years, ever since her mother passed away, it had just been the two of them.

"I've never ridden at night before." She picked up Daisy, hugged her, kissed her on the head and then set her down gently on the porch.

Hunter put one boot on the bottom step, leaned forward, held out his hand to her and said, "Our first date should be memorable."

"A moonlight ride." She took his hand. It was the most romantic of first dates. How many women got to say that they rode horses with a dreamy cowboy during a full moon? This would be a moment seared into her heart forever, she was certain of that. Jeremy had actually been a very romantic boyfriend, but not even he could manage a moonlight ride in Montana.

He held on to her hand as they took their time walking to the barn; the air was so clean and crisp that she had to breathe it in deeply several times.

"Are you okay?" Hunter asked.

"I'm perfect." She sighed. "The air smells so good right now."

She saw Hunter take a couple of small sniffs of the air out of her peripheral vision.

"It does?"

She laughed, "Yes. It does. It smells like a Christmas candle. Like pine and wood."

Hunter squeezed her hand in an affectionate gesture. "I don't smell all that, but if you do, and you like it, then I'm glad."

"I do and I do," she said and then breathed in deeply again.

Hunter gave her a leg up on Dream Catcher's back; she had ridden regularly since she had been in Montana, which allowed her to feel more comfortable and confident in the saddle. Recently, her inner thigh muscles had stopped being sore and most of the blisters on her feet had cleared up. Lately, she had been walking like a normal human instead of a rickety robot bolted together by rusty nails.

"Wow," she said, knowing that she still used that word way too much. But how else could she describe the feeling of being on Dream Catcher's back with only the light of the moon to guide her?

"It's a different feeling, isn't it?" Hunter rode up beside her on Zodiac.

"If I could be speechless, I would be speechless right now," she said, her heart beginning to race with excitement and nervousness. "What if there's something out there that spooks the horses?"

"You can handle it," he responded, trying to reassure her. "I wouldn't risk this if I thought you would get injured."

He had been very protective of her ever since she passed out on the first day. If Hunter believed that she could do this, then she had to find a way to believe in her own ability, too.

Hunter pointed Zodiac toward a familiar trail, one that they had ridden together many times. It was so different riding in the dark; her eyes had adjusted and she could make out the basic shape of Hunter's body astride Zodiac up ahead. Through the branches of the trees and the thick summer leaves, flashes of that buttery yellow light from the full moon filtered through, looking like a black-and-gold kaleidoscope that changed and shifted and morphed into something even more beautiful with every step Dream

Catcher took. Because of her inability to use her sight, her other senses were heightened. She was keenly aware of the sounds around her—the creaking of the leather, the soft brushing of her jeans against the saddle, the distinctive sound of Dream Catcher's hooves as they hit the ground and the cracking of dried twigs as they snapped beneath the pressure of the horses' hooves.

"You okay back there?" She saw Hunter as a black outline, which changed as he turned his head to look back at her. "You're awfully quiet."

"I feel like I'm in church. Like I need to whisper."

"You do feel a bit closer to God out here, like this," he agreed.

Skyler rested the hand holding the reins on the saddle horn and the other on her thigh. She worked to relax her torso, letting the natural rhythm of the horse's walking gait move her hips back and forward.

"I want to close my eyes," she said quietly.

"Then do it," Hunter said. "Dream knows where to go. Trust her to take care of you."

Skyler followed her instincts and closed her eyes. It felt like she was engaging in one of those trust-building exercises that her company sponsored every year—where she would have to allow herself to fall backward into the awaiting hands of her coworkers, trusting that they wouldn't let her fall.

"Ah." She breathed out the sound of wonder. "I hear so much more—I *feel* so much more."

She mapped the trail in her mind and knew that they were approaching a corner. After the corner, a small bridge would take them over a stream. Skyler heard the water rushing over the rocks, gurgling and bubbling, and then she heard Zodiac's hooves *clop, clop, clop* on the wood of the bridge. Skyler opened her eyes and blinked several times, trying to hurry up the process of adjusting her eyes. Her eyes adjusted just in time for her to see the edge of the railing for the bridge, and down below the bridge, glimpses of white as the water rushed by. Never in her life had she experienced this feeling of innate freedom, joy, empowerment and bliss. She was smiling broadly and her soul felt like singing. She was happy, content and so grateful to Hunter for always pushing her in the best way.

She wanted to share the feeling with him. "I feel so happy."

She heard Hunter chuckle. "So far I'm not doing too bad for our first date."

That was an understatement—how could any man in her future top this? They would have to rent out the top of the Empire State Building or something outrageous like that. She didn't share this fact with Hunter—no sense laying it on too thick. It was enough that she knew that this was a highlight of her life. Not even in her wildest teenage imaginings of her first date with *the* Hunter Brand from *Cowboy Up!* had she imagined this.

At the edge of the trail, they entered a clearing and the full moon came into view. In the expansive Montana sky, the moon loomed so large and bright that she reached out her hand to touch it.

Hunter stopped Zodiac so she could pull beside him. "This is what I wanted you to see."

Her hand on her heart, she felt tears come to her eyes at the beauty she was bearing witness to. First her mother had been diagnosed with congestive heart failure, changing the course of her life. She had quit college, taken a job with Molly at a nationwide insurance company and done her best to take care of her mother until her dying day. And just when she thought she had gotten her life stable and her father was sort of back to some semblance of normalcy, they were both thrown back into the fight by her cancer diagnosis. A lung cancer caused by a genetic mutation in young adults, like her, who'd never touched a cigarette.

Tears rolled unchecked down her cheeks and she tried to hide them from Hunter, but a telltale catch in her breathing brought his attention to her.

"Skyler?" He said her name with a concerned undertone. "Are you crying?"

Skyler wiped her tears away with her hand and nodded wordlessly.

"What's wrong? What did I do?"

She shook her head. "You didn't do anything wrong, Hunter. I'm not crying because I'm sad. I'm crying because I'm happy."

"Happy crying?"

The way he asked the question, as if he had asked about something so confusing and foreign to him that he could have been asking her about an alien landing, made her laugh through her tears.

"It happens. To me at least," she explained. "Glorious things make me cry."

Hunter reached for her hand; she put her hand into his, noting the rough patch on his palm where a callus had developed. She had forgotten her gloves and he had given her his; that callus was one of the results of that gesture of care he had shown her. She rubbed her thumb over that callus like she would a worry stone, and they sat together, basking in the light of the moon, while she silently added this special moment to her ever-growing list of blessings.

"Are you ready to move on?" he asked her quietly after many minutes had ticked by. "There's more I want to show you."

Hunter led her to a field of fireflies—acres and acres of tiny green lights blinking like nature's very own holiday decoration.

"Christmas in July," Skyler said in wonder.

"I've never thought of it that way before."

"It reminds me of holiday lights. But there are thousands and thousands of them."

After the field of fireflies, he turned them back into the woods, taking them on the familiar path for her comfort. He always seemed mindful of her experience of his world; he always wanted her to feel safe and secure with him. And she did. She truly did.

"What is that smell?" Skyler closed her eyes for a moment to focus on her nose. "Vanilla! It smells like a sugar cookie. What is that?!"

"Clematis." She could hear the pleasure in his voice. He had surprised her again and he was enjoying his success. "They bloom in late spring and early summer. We have caught them just in time. Soon the scent will be gone."

They ended their moonlight ride at Hunter's stake, Oak Tree Hill. They let the horses graze nearby as they walked, hand and hand, by the light of the moon, to the grand, overarching ancient canopies that were the crowning glory of the property.

"I thought I would start a campfire. Maybe make some s'mores."

"Do you make a mental note of everything I say?" She laughed and leaned into his body. She had mentioned wanting to make s'mores and now it was coming true. It really did seem like to her that Hunter was trying to make all of her Montana dreams come true.

"I try," he said a bit sheepishly.

"You succeed, Hunter," she said, squeezing his hand. She found a comfortable spot on a bench carved from a log harvested from one of the oak trees that had died. Hunter had cut down that tree with his own hands and then carved a lovely bench for his fire from it.

The bench had a sweet, woody scent and was smooth to the touch as she ran her hands over the surface. Hunter had taken much care with the bench; it was a piece of art, really.

Hunter kneeled down by the firepit, tossed some kindling on the fire and then struck a match and tossed it onto the kindling. He joined her on the two-seater bench; he took her hand and, silently, they watched the fire grow.

"I love this bench," she said to him. "It's actually comfortable."

"You're the first person to sit on it with me."

She looked at him, surprised. "That's not true, is it?"

He nodded, staring into the fire. "I wouldn't lie to you."

"I feel…" She searched her mind for the correct feeling. "Honored."

Then, to break the mood, as she'd always tried to do with her father when her mother was at her sickest, she added, "And hungry. Honored and hungry."

Her attempt at humor had the desired effect—the cowboy laughed. "Let me go grab the fixin's." He stood up. "Don't go anywhere."

She lifted her arms and looked around. "Where am I going to go? I'm a captive audience."

"Exactly." He grinned at her mischievously.

Looking at Hunter never got old; she loved everything that made him *him*—the cleft in his chin, the black-brown hair that he kept cropped short, the strong, straight nose and those sexy, intense, ocean-blue eyes. He had only gotten more handsome with age, and every time—every single time—she looked at him, she felt her heart thump a little bit harder. What she couldn't quite figure is what exactly he wanted with her.

She had always felt puppy love for this man— at least the TV version of him. Now she had a full-blown adult crush on him that was an undeniable fact. But Hunter having feelings for her beyond friendship didn't make logical sense to her. And that wasn't to say that she didn't feel worthy; her illness had given her the gift of self-esteem. She admired her own strength and she was grateful for the vessel she occupied, albeit petite and flat-chested with oddly colored hair that was now sprouting back out of her scalp. She liked herself...she loved herself. She fought the negative demons like anyone else, but she had a keen appreciation for who she was and what she brought to any relationship. And still, Hunter Brand's interest was a bit of a mystery. She realized now that she was a bit more of city mouse than a country mouse; she was like a

hothouse flower found in a field of wildflowers—
beautiful but oddly placed.

"Graham crackers, chocolate, marshmallows."

"What else could a girl want?" She clasped her
hands together in front of her.

"A little company from a cowboy?" He sat down
beside her and put the food on the ground in front
of them.

"Okay." She smiled and laughed. "That, too."

They had laughed for hours together up on his hill.
Hunter couldn't remember laughing with a woman
the way he laughed with Skyler. She amused him;
she challenged him. She made him think. And she
made him see his world through a different lens—a
lens that he was beginning to like very much.

"How come I'm always stuffing my face around
you?" Skyler put her hands on her stomach with
a groan. "I swear I've never acted so much like a
swine in front of anyone else."

"You have no idea how much I love that about
you," Hunter said. "A ranch woman needs to eat to
keep up her strength."

Skyler sat up a little straighter, her chin raised.
"A ranch woman. I'm adding that to my résumé."

"You should."

"Cow wormer." She laughed. "Fence tearer-downer."

"You've developed a whole new skill set in a short
amount of time." He leaned forward to stoke the fire.

"I really have! I'm not sure how handy this will be in the customer-service arena when my leave of absence is over." She shrugged with a self-effacing smile. "But you never know what life might bring."

Hunter sat back. "Customer service. That doesn't really seem like you."

"I think I'll have just one more," she said when she saw him packing up the food.

He smiled as he skewered two of the giant marshmallows on the stick and held it over the fire to toast. "I'm going to make you the best s'more of the evening."

Skyler rubbed her knees with her hands in anticipation. "I don't mind my job, really. I get to help people resolve their problems. I get yelled at a lot, but those are the ones I feel most proud of when they hang up the phone because I feel like I really cared about finding a solution for them." She addressed his earlier comment about her job. "I took what I could get when I quit college. Mom was sick and Dad needed to keep working full-time at the garage so they wouldn't lose their medical benefits. My income helped make a dent in some of the bills."

Her voice softened a bit at the memory. "I don't regret it—leaving college. I got to be there for the most important woman in my life and I got to be there for my dad, too."

Hunter wanted to ask her about her mother's illness, but she hadn't offered it and he decided not to pry.

"Do you ever think of going back? To college?" he asked instead while he pressed the perfectly toasted marshmallows on top of four squares of milk chocolate and two pieces of graham crackers. He stuck his creation back over the fire to melt the chocolate and then quickly removed it.

"Actually, I had already been accepted to the City College of New York for premedical studies and then—" she shrugged "—my body had other plans for me."

Hunter wished he knew the right words to say when Skyler shared something so personal with him, and yet he didn't. He felt woefully inadequate when it came to feelings and emotions. His special skill set was distraction and deflection. So that's what he did now.

"Madam—" he presented the s'more to Skyler "—your dessert is served."

"My dessert for after my dessert?"

He loved the sound of her laugh, the way her smile always reached her wide, unusual blue-lavender eyes. Perhaps that was her special appeal to him: she did everything to the fullest, even smiling. Even laughing.

"Mmmm." Skyler's eyes got even bigger after the first bite. She had marshmallow and chocolate on the corner of her mouth and it was still there after she popped in the final bite.

"That was the best s'more of my life," she told him.

Acting on impulse, Hunter kissed the corner of her mouth, tasting the sweetness of the marshmallow and chocolate.

Skyler's eyes widened again and she edged away from him for the briefest of moments before she leaned in toward him and kissed him on the lips. He slipped his hand behind her neck and deepened the kiss. He caught her breath in his mouth, tasted the sweetness on her tongue.

"I like the way you taste," he murmured against her lips.

"I like the way you smell." Skyler scooted closer to him, pressing her small, pert breasts against his body. He wanted to touch her; he wanted to feel the silkiness of her skin. She was soft in all of the places he wanted to fill with his hardness.

He easily scooped her up and put her on his lap. He knew, without any doubt, that she could feel his desire for her. Skyler leaned her body into him, took his face in her hands and returned his kisses.

He didn't want to go too far. He *didn't* want to go too fast. But, God, he didn't want to stop. She was so light and airy in his arms; her kisses were so sweet and sincere. He wanted more of Skyler—he wanted her for always.

Chapter Nine

Always. The last thought that came into his mind—
the thought of forever had the same effect as if someone had thrown a bucket of ice water on his head.

Hunter stood up with her in his arms, gently set
her down on her feet and took a step back from her.
In the process, he almost fell backward over the log
bench he had carved for two.

Skyler looked as stunned and confused as he felt.

"I don't want to ruin this by going too fast, Skyler."

She nodded. "I've always been the tortoise, not
the hare."

His body was still hard and aching for her, and
he willed the bulge in his pants to go down.

"Do you mind if I use your bathroom?" she asked. "My hands are all sticky."

"Be my guest."

He was grateful that she left him in that moment; he shifted his erection in his pants and felt relieved that it was starting to subside. He had always wanted to be a married man, but he had never found a woman who made him want to commit. In his heart, he had always known it would be a woman born in Montana, raised on a cattle ranch, like he'd been. How could Skyler—a spritelike woman from New York, be making him think of forever for the first time? Could Skyler really fit in with ranch life for the long haul? Would she last decades of harsh Montana winters, with one day running into the next without a break from the work? This life wasn't a vacation and there was rarely an opportunity to have a vacation from the life.

"Thank you." Skyler reappeared with a shy smile on her face, her arms intertwined like a pretzel in front of her body.

While she was in his trailer, he had doused the fire and laid out a blanket for them to admire the moon. He wasn't ready to ride back to the cabin; he wasn't ready for the night to end. He hoped she felt the same way.

"Come join me." He gestured to the blanket. "We'll let our food settle before we ride back."

"I like that plan."

She joined him on the blanket and they lay on their backs, looking up at the full moon above. They held hands, their shoulders and their booted feet touching.

"This was the best first date of my life," she whispered.

"This was the best first date of my life," he replied, echoing the sentiment.

After a while, she curled on her side, rested her head on his shoulder and her hand over his heart. He breathed in the scent of her and hugged her more closely to his body as her breathing changed and he realized she had fallen asleep in his arms. The end of summer would arrive eventually How would he ever be able to let his quirky, enchanting angel go?

Skyler awoke with a crick in her neck and a pain in her back from a jagged rock under the blanket.

"Oh." She winced as she sat upright, blinking her eyes against the daylight. She hadn't slept this late since the first week at the ranch.

"Hunter?" Skyler looked around, wincing every time she turned her neck to the right too far. She stood up stiffly, holding her neck, and continued to look around.

"Hunter?" The fire was going in the pit and there was a pot of coffee cooking, so he couldn't have gone too far.

Just then, the door to the trailer swung open and

a refreshed Hunter came through the door balancing a load of eggs, bacon and biscuits.

"Good morning." He shot her that famous, dimpled smile of his. "How'd you sleep?"

"Like a rock." She leaned backward to stretch out the kinks. "And literally *on* a rock."

He laughed and squatted down, setting a well-worn cast-iron skillet on a grate over the fire.

"I didn't have the heart to wake you last night." He poured her a cup of coffee. "Black is the best I can do."

Skyler hunkered down on the bench, wiped the sleep out of her eyes and yawned while holding the tin cup filled with steaming coffee in her free hand. "Wow. That's a first. Sleeping outside under the stars."

In the arms of my dream cowboy.

"Did I snore?" she asked.

"Not really." He cracked the eggs into the skillet. "But you do talk in your sleep."

"I do not."

"Find me a bible." He winked at her with a grin.

"Okay." She slurped the hot coffee, hating the bitter taste but wanting the caffeine to wake her up. "What did I say?"

"Mumble, mumble, mumble... Hunter."

She stopped slurping, her mouth hanging open. "No. I. Did. Not."

"You did." He took a spatula and started to scramble the eggs.

"And, of course, you had to tell me."

"Heck yeah." He laughed, shifting his weight. "Great ego boost for me."

She took another sip of the coffee. "Do you really need an ego boost, Hunter?"

Hunter smiled at her with another wink. "Everyone can use a good ego boost, every now and again. Even washed-up reality TV stars."

Skyler was surprised that he brought up the show; he had always reacted so badly when she mentioned it that she had stopped mentioning *Cowboy Up!* entirely out of respect for his feelings.

"Especially washed-up reality TV stars," he added as an aside.

"Maybe I said, 'hunt.' Maybe I was dreaming about being on a safari." She put her coffee cup on the ground.

"No." He gave a little shake of his head. "It was 'Hunter,' loud and clear."

"Fine, *Hunter*," she said, overemphasizing his name as she stood up. "Mind if I use your bathroom?"

"Mi casa es tu casa." He kept right on cooking the eggs.

By the time she returned, he had cooked up the eggs, the bacon and the biscuits in the same skillet,

and she felt more human for having washed her face
and rinsed out her mouth with mouthwash.

"Hmm. Smells good." She returned to her spot,
her stomach growling in response to the delicious
smells emanating from the campfire.

"Gonna taste good, too."

He handed her a plate and fork and she dived
right in. Hunter always made her feel good about
her appetite—it was something that reminded her
of her father.

"What about all of our morning chores?" she
asked between bites.

"I put a call in to Bruce—he took care of it."

"It's twenty-four seven here, isn't it?"

Hunter nodded while he chewed. "That's the life."

"A hard life," Skyler noted, putting her empty plate
on the bench next to her. "It's not like I imagined."

It seemed that Hunter's body stiffened beside her,
but he didn't say anything in response; he just listened to her.

"Where are the horses?" Skyler suddenly sat
more upright, looking around. "Did they run away?"

Hunter finished his breakfast, stood up and
stacked her plate on top of his. "They're probably
on the other side of those trees."

"I think I'll take a walk. See if I can spot them.
Okay with you?"

"Do your thing." Hunter headed toward the
trailer. "I'll meet you out there after I clean up."

"Would you rather I help you?"

"I've got this."

"Okay." She stood up. "Thank you for breakfast. You are an excellent fireside cook."

"I'll have to teach you."

"That would be a neat trick. My father wouldn't believe it."

While she walked through the field, running her hand over the tips of the tall grass, watching where she was stepping to avoid snakes or other creatures, her father was on her mind. She missed him; when she returned to the cabin, she would call him for a long chat.

She stopped to take pictures of the landscape, always wanting to keep her social media updated with new content for all of the people who were following her on her journey. Many of the people who had donated to make this trip possible were "liking" and commenting on her pictures and videos. It made her feel connected to home; it made her feel connected to all of those people who had sacrificed something—even if it had been a dollar—to make her dream come true.

"There you are!" She stopped and snapped photographs of Zodiac and Dream Catcher nibbling on some leaves from some fallen branches.

After she got the picture she wanted, she walked more quickly toward her equine friends. She had grown to love them both and was happy to see that they'd fared well overnight.

Dream Catcher saw her, nickered and walked toward her, no doubt hoping that Skyler would have a molasses treat in her pocket. Zodiac slowly followed the mare and that's when Skyler noticed something odd about Zodiac's gait. He was walking oddly, swinging his head to the right while his left hind leg was swinging outward. The only thing that popped into her mind was that he looked drunk.

"Oh, no." Her stomach clenched. She ran up to meet him. "What's wrong, Zodiac? What's wrong with you?"

She checked his legs and didn't see any sign that a snake had bitten him—the skin wasn't broken and there wasn't any swelling. But there was definitely something seriously wrong with him. Shaking with nerves, she fished her phone out of her pocket and tried to call Hunter.

"Pick up! Pick up!" she yelled at the phone. "Damn it, Hunter! Pick up the phone!"

When he didn't answer the phone, she gave up and started to run toward the campsite. Like her US Marine father had taught her, in order to cover long distances without tiring out, she jogged fifty steps and then speed-walked fifty steps, over and over again, until she was in yelling distance of the trailer.

"Hunter!" she gasped, holding her side and out of breath. "Hunter!"

The cowboy came out of the trailer; he must have spotted her.

"What's wrong?" He raced to her side.

"Zodiac! There's something wrong with him. He's walking like he's drunk. Did he have a stroke? Can a horse have a stroke?"

"No. They aren't built that way," Hunter said as he helped her over to the bench and made sure she was settled. Then he grabbed his phone, which he'd left by the campfire, and called his brother Liam, who was a large-animal veternarian.

"I may need you out here ASAP," he said into the phone. "Where are you now?"

Skyler watched Hunter's face carefully while he spoke to his brother. After a moment, Hunter nodded his head.

"Just be on standby for me, brother. I'm going to see if I can lead him back to camp. Could be snakebit."

Hunter ended the call and she watched him grab a lead rope. "Liam is thirty minutes away. I want you to stay right here and wait for me."

Skyler put her head in her hands and prayed for Zodiac. "Please, God. Please. Please let Zodiac be okay. *Please*."

Hunter made his way to the horses as quickly as he could. The way Skyler had described Zodiac's behavior made him immediately alarmed. She wasn't one for hysterics or exaggeration. There was something seriously wrong with Zodiac, and from past experience Hunter knew there was no guarantee that he would survive.

"Hey, boy." Hunter approached Zodiac cautiously. The horse was still grazing, so that was a plus. If the horse was still eating and defecating, that was a sign that his systems were still functioning somewhat normally.

Hunter hooked the lead rope to the horse's halter and coaxed him forward. When the horse took an awkward, disjointed couple of steps forward, Hunter immediately saw what Skyler had described.

"What the hell?" He searched Zodiac's body, looking for swelling or a sign of snakebite, but he couldn't find anything.

"Come on, bubba." Hunter started the long walk back to the campsite. Dream Catcher kept on grazing, but when they got too far away for her liking the mare snorted and trotted after them.

Skyler met them halfway. "What's wrong?"

"I'm not sure," he confessed, wishing he had a better answer. "Stay back away from him."

She listened to him and backed away from the gelding that was still walking with an odd gait, throwing his head to the right and his left hind leg outward.

"I need to help," Skyler said to him.

"Get Dream Catcher's lead rope and ground-tie

her." Hunter understood her need to keep busy. He pulled his phone out of his pocket and called Liam.

"Bring your trailer," Hunter told him. "Get here as soon as you can."

Hunter shot a quick video of Zodiac walking and texted it to Liam.

"He's coming?"

Hunter nodded. "Now all we can do is wait."

"And pray."

He rubbed his hand over his forehead and down his face. She was right about that. All they could do was wait and pray. But Hunter had a bad feeling in his gut. He didn't share his thoughts with Skyler, but there was no way to predict if Zodiac would ever make it back to base camp.

Liam was taller, blonder and had a lighter complexion, but the eyes were the exact same ocean-blue as Hunter's eyes.

"Did you see anything out in the field?" Liam had dropped everything to come to their aid.

"No." Hunter shook his head. "Not that I could see. Not anything that would cause this."

"They were just eating some leaves off of dead branches when I first saw them." Skyler stood away from Zodiac as Hunter had asked her to do.

Both Liam and Hunter snapped their heads up and looked at her. "What branches?" Hunter asked.

"They were over at the edge of the woods," she explained. "They were both eating them."

"Damn." Hunter exchanged a look with his brother.

"Can you show us the branches?" Liam asked her.

Liam rolled the windows down in his truck and they rode together through the field to the edge of the woods.

"Right there." She pointed to the felled branches.

"Is that a cherry tree?" Hunter pointed to a large tree to the left of the branches.

"I think so." Liam shut off the engine and hopped out of the truck.

Skyler followed the men a couple of paces back. Hunter and his brother examined the branches and the leaves.

"The wind must've knocked these branches loose." Liam looked up at the tree. "The leaves are fairly fresh."

"Damn." This was Hunter's response.

"What is it?" she asked impatiently, not understanding what the tree limbs or the leaves had to do with Zodiac's drunken state.

Hunter and Liam headed back to where she was standing.

"Zodiac was eating those leaves?" Liam asked. "You're sure?"

She nodded. "Both of them were."

"But Dream Catcher is fine," Hunter pointed out.

"Maybe she only ate the branches, not the leaves," Liam countered.

"Will you *please* tell me what's going on?" Skyler raised her voice to gain their attention.

"That's a cherry tree," Liam explained. "If the limbs are disturbed..."

"The leaves produce arsenic."

"Cyanide?!" Skyler exclaimed. "Like the poison? *That* cyanide?"

Hunter nodded, his face grim.

Skyler followed them back to the truck, her gut churning with acid and upset. Nothing in Liam's or Hunter's demeanor gave her comfort.

"What does this mean for Zodiac?" she asked.

"I'm not sure," Liam told her with honesty ringing in his tone. "Most of these horses are found dead in the pasture."

Skyler had to swallow back bile that jumped up her throat. She pressed her hands onto her stomach and closed her eyes.

"And the others?" she asked, knowing that she might not like the unvarnished truth she was about to receive from Liam.

"The others are usually put down because they are too dangerous. They can't control their body and could accidentally kill anybody nearby."

"Oh, God." The words tumbled out of her mouth.

Hunter reached back behind the seat, grabbed her

hand and squeezed her fingers. "Liam isn't saying that we're there yet."

"Not yet." Liam stopped the truck, shut off the engine and they all jumped out. "We need to see if we can get him in the trailer. If we can, I'll take him to Triple K so I can keep a closer eye on him."

"You're not just taking him away to put him down, are you?" Skyler was shaking with adrenaline and fear.

"No." Liam looked her dead in the eye. "If we have to put him down, we will tell you."

They tried for an hour to get Zodiac in the trailer. He was normally an "easy loader," according to Hunter, but he wouldn't load.

"His perception is too far off. He doesn't trust his own footing," Liam said. "We can try to lead him back to the cabin or we can treat him here."

"I don't have a shelter in place. No water other than the stream down there by the cherry tree," Hunter countered.

"Then we've got to walk him back," Liam said. "That's the best of the bad choices I'm afraid."

It was an arduous journey back to the cabin. Skyler road Dream Catcher and brought up the rear while Hunter led Zodiac in the lead position. It was painful to watch Zodiac swerving and lurching, uncertain of his footing. They stopped often, grateful that the gelding was still interested in eating and drinking; he had also stopped to relieve himself. Taken together, there was some reason to be hopeful. Skyler had learned that holding on to hope mattered. In fact, it could save a life. It had hers.

It was a relief to see the cabin come into view. They had made it. Zodiac had made it so far. Hunter got the gelding into his stall while Skyler untacked Dream Catcher, rinsed her off with the hose and then put her in her stall. Soon after they arrived, Liam came down from the main house.

"I've made some calls and I've done some research."

Standing next to Hunter, she waited to hear the news.

"No one really knows what to do in this situation. Like I said, most horses don't make it this far."

"Zodiac is a miracle horse," she interjected.

"So far," Liam agreed, but his tone was tempered and cautious. "There is a medicine that has been reported in the literature to work, but I've called around and I can't get my hands on it."

Liam continued. "There have been some studies that report some therapeutic success of vitamin B12 helping if the case of poisoning is mild and caught early."

"That sounds like us." Hunter had his arms crossed, his legs braced apart.

"I can give him B12 and we'll keep him in the stall for now."

"No pasture time?" Hunter asked.

"For now," Liam said. "We are in unchartered territory here. That's all I can say."

Liam treated Zodiac and then left them with a promise to return the next day to check on him and give him another round of B12. Skyler hung over the stall gate, not wanting to leave the handsome gelding alone.

Hunter came up behind her and put his hands on her shoulders. "I'm going to hang around for the next couple of days. There's a cot in Liam's shop."

Skyler turned in his arms, wrapped her arms around his waist and rested her head on his chest, comforted by the strong beat of his heart. Hunter held her tightly in his arms and kissed the top of her head.

"You will stay in the cabin," she told him.

"If that's what you want."

She wrapped her arms more tightly around his body and closed her eyes. "Do you think he will be all right, Hunter?"

"I don't know, Skyler." She could count on Hunter to tell her the truth even if she wanted to hear a lie. "We will just have to wait and see."

Chapter Ten

That night, Hunter had to insist that she leave the barn to get some rest. "Zodiac needs you to be strong for him."

Skyler rubbed the gelding's neck one last time and pressed a kiss on his velvety soft nose. "I will see you in the morning. You will feel better tomorrow. And everyone will know that you are a miracle horse."

"I'm going to let you sleep in tomorrow morning." Hunter had his arm around her waist.

"I do think I need to rest."

"Do not go into Zodiac's stall, Skyler. Promise me. He wouldn't mean to hurt you."

"I won't," she said. "I promise."

They took turns in the single bathroom, each showering off the dirt of the day. They ate a quiet meal, both too tired and too worried to banter. Hunter found some extra pillows and bedding inside an old leather steamer trunk that pulled double duty as a coffee table. While Skyler washed the dishes, Hunter made up the couch.

"I've got to get some sleep." Hunter yawned, his eyes heavy lidded.

She stepped into his arms and hugged him goodnight.

"You won't be mad if I go to bed so early?"

"No." She left his embrace. "You need to get your rest."

Meowing at the door caught Skyler's attention. She hurried to the door and opened it to find Daisy on the other side.

"Where have you been?" Skyler bent down and scooped up the cat. "I have been worried sick about you."

She made sure that Daisy had water and food before she came back inside the house. Hunter had removed his shirt and was lying on the couch, covered by a sheet up to his torso.

"Do you think that Liam would mind if Daisy came inside the cabin? I hate for her to be outside by herself at night."

"You can ask him tomorrow. I'm pretty sure he'll say yes."

Skyler got into bed, turned off the light and stared up at the ceiling. She was exhausted and wide-awake. An hour ticked by and she had tossed and turned until her blanket and sheets were tangled around her legs. Frustrated, she kicked and kicked until she was free. Quietly, she padded out to the kitchen to get a cold glass of water.

"You can't sleep?" Hunter asked the question in the dark and gave her a start.

"You scared me." She filled a glass with water and drank it down. "I thought you were asleep."

"No." He sat up and leaned forward, resting his head in his hands. "This couch is killing my back."

Skyler put the glass on the counter. This was ridiculous. She couldn't sleep; he couldn't sleep. They were both adults. It didn't make sense that they should be apart.

"Come to bed," she said.

Hunter lifted his head and looked over at her. She breathed in, held it and then let out a breath slowly, awaiting his response.

"Skyler, if I come to bed with you, we will end up making love," he said with the honesty she had come to expect from him.

How many seconds slipped by while she absorbed his words. She knew he spoke the truth and her next words would decide the path that their relationship would take. She knew what she wanted—she wanted to be with Hunter, even if they only had the summer.

She put the empty glass in the sink, walked to the couch, held out her hand for him to take and said, "Come to bed with me, cowboy."

Her bravery waned when she found herself alone with Hunter in the cabin bedroom. Out in the living room, she had felt empowered, like a woman in charge of her own sexuality. Once in the bedroom, the lights thankfully off, and *the* cowboy of her dreams outlined by the dim light streaming in through the window by the bed, she faltered.

"Having second thoughts?" he asked her, standing shirtless by the bed.

"No," she whispered. Then, after a moment, she said, "Yes."

Hunter walked over to where she was standing in the doorway, cupped his hand around the back of her neck and kissed the top of her head.

"There're bunk beads in the spare room. I'll sleep there."

"No." She caught his hand. "That room is full of boxes. It's like a storage room. You'd have to move things around just to get to the beds."

"Then I'll go back to the couch," he said. "I don't want you worrying about me. I've slept on the ground working cattle than in a bed."

Skyler grabbed his hand and held on to it.

"I'm serious," he said, trying to reassure her. "This is too fast. You're the tortoise, remember?"

Hunter was doing his level best to make her feel comfortable in an awkward situation. But he was getting it all wrong. She wanted to be the hare; for once in her life, she was determined to be the hare.

"I don't want you to go."

He leaned down and touched his forehead to hers. "I don't think you know what you want right now, Skyler. And that's okay. I don't want you to wake up with regrets. I just know that if I get into the bed with you, I'm going to need to touch you."

Skyler lifted her head so her lips naturally touched his. She lifted up on her tiptoes, put her hands on either side of his face and kissed him. Hunter looped his arm around her back and pulled her tightly into his body. He could lift her and hold her against him with one arm—the strength of the man made her feel womanly. The soapy, clean scent of his warm skin and the feel of this bicep flexing against her back as he held her close to him were heady sensations. The kissed deepened as her breathing became shallow and quick.

"Tell me what to do." Hunter kissed her neck right below her ear.

She shuddered with pleasure, her eyes closed, her fingers in his hair.

"What do you want?" His face was pressed into her neck.

"I want you to stay with me." She raked her fingers through his hair. "I want you to make love to me."

No words from the cowboy, just kisses—on her neck, her chin—and then his strong, firm lips found her softer lips.

"I don't...." She moved her head back an inch or two so she could tell be as honest with him as she thought he was being with her. "I don't feel sexy."

Hunter stopped trying to kiss her and straightened his arms so there was a little distance between them.

"What?" He genuinely sounded surprised. Confused.

"My hair," she said. "My body in general, I suppose. I just don't feel...like *myself* yet."

Hunter stared down at her face, his eyes appearing almost black in the darkened room. "Do I have some say in this?"

When she didn't respond, he asked the question again. "Do I have a say in this?"

"I don't know," she said. "What do you want to say?"

Hunter slipped his hands down, cupped her bottom and pulled her upward into his body. "I think you're sexy, Skyler."

Their groins were pressed tightly together now and she could feel Hunter's rock-hard erection; her body responded with a more intense ache. The moment she felt it, she wanted it. She wanted to touch it, hold it, kiss it. She wanted to get it inside her, sink down on it.

"I think you're *very* sexy, Skyler." Hunter suddenly lifted her up in the air and she naturally wrapped her legs around his waist. He walked them back a couple of feet to the nearby wall and pressed her against it, his hard-on hitting the bull's-eye on her body. He grabbed her arms, lifted them above her head, linked their fingers together and kissed her hard and long.

"Tell me that you believe me." Hunter stopped kissing her and held his lips away from her even as she leaned her head forward, trying to recapture his mouth with hers.

"Tell me." He thrust his hips into hers and she wanted—*needed*—to rip away the layers of material separating their flesh.

"I believe you," she gasped, desiring him like she had never desired another man. She was in pain, a pleasurable, exquisite, throbbing pain she had never known existed before. "I believe you."

With one arm secured around her back, he let her slide down his body until her feet were touching the ground. He kneeled down before her, running his hands down to her backside, then hooked his fingers in the waistband of her simple white cotton panties. She was sure he was going to pull off those panties; she wanted him to rip them off, bite them off, get them off as quickly as he could. But he didn't. He teased her, kissing her mound through the thin material, making her push her body toward his lips, moaning and holding on to his head to keep herself upright on legs that felt like they were made of Jell-O.

Hunter slipped his hands—such large, strong hands—under the short nightie she was wearing, lifting it as he went. He stood up and kept right on lifting the nightie until she had a choice—stop his progression or raise her arms. Slowly, languidly, feeling dazed with so many wondrous sensations bursting all over her body, she raised her arms.

Hunter smiled—she saw the flash of his white teeth—as he freed her from her simple, unremark-able nightgown.

Her chest rising and falling from passion, and with a strip of light illuminating her left breast and the nipple that was tight and hard, Hunter stared at her chest just as she was staring at his.

"You are incredibly beautiful." The cowboy traced the side of her small, pert breast with his finger. "The rarest of flowers."

She caught his hand and pressed it over her breast, closing her eyes at the feeling of his warm palm on her skin.

One hand still on her breast, his thumb gently worrying her nipple, Hunter's free hand cupped the back of her head and he kissed her again. She opened her mouth as she intended to open her body to him. Hunter lifted her with ease and carried her to the bed. She watched as he stripped off his jeans and his underwear. He was unabashed in his nakedness—strong, muscled thighs, corded abs, a beautiful defined chest and a thick, magnificent, hard cock.

Skyler reached for him, heard him gasp with pleasure and surprise. She put him in his mouth, something she knew she would do, and heard him groan at the feeling of her tongue on his skin.

He let her take her time with him, explore him, feel him, dominate him. And then, when she had taken him right to the edge of no return, Hunter stripped off her panties, kneeled down on the ground between her thighs and turned her into a midnight snack.

"Oh, my God." She grabbed the blanket on the best in her fists. "Oh, my God."

"No." The cowboy kissed the inside of her thigh. "Hunter."

"Hunter," she moaned. "Hunter. Hunter."

By the time he was done with her, she was screaming his name, grateful that there were miles of woods between them and another living soul. After he brought her up to the top of the mountain, and she'd shouted his name to the rooftops, Hunter hovered his body above hers.

"I have to go get a condom," he said regretfully.

"The drawer." She flung her hand weakly toward the nightstand. "The top drawer."

Hunter looked at her, surprised, as he reached across her and fished a condom out of the drawer.

The wrapper was soon on the floor, the condom secured, and the cowboy was all the way inside her, making her gasp and arch her back. He knew how to love a woman's body and she just held on for the ride. His movements were long, slow, deep, and he nibbled her ear, sucked on her nipple.

"You're about to come," he whispered in her ear. How did he know? How could he know?

He pushed deeply into her one more time, his hand beneath her bottom, and then stopped and let her take control of her own destiny. She writhed against him, panting, straining, using him just the way her body needed, until the wave, that glorious wave, crashed over her, again and again, and again.

Hunter had watched her take her pleasure; he was her witness. She opened her eyes, saw him watching her, and to his surprise, she didn't look away. Instead, she watched him. She watched him as he pushed into her body, faster, harder, doing what his body needed…what it craved. He threw back his head and growled loudly as the climax ripped through him. He hadn't felt this before—this intensity, this satisfaction. This love.

They were breathing heavily, their bodies still connected, the air feeling cool against their hot skin.

"Why?" Skyler asked with an emotional catch in her throat.

He understood what she was asking. Why did he do everything in his power to make her happy? Why did he always try to make her every dream, no matter how small, come true? Why had he just made love to her with every fiber of his being? Why he had loved her like he was on a mission to spoil her for every other man who had a thought to touch her?

Hunter lifted his head, closed his eyes and tried to catch his breath. Then, staring deeply into her lovely eyes, he said, "Because I love you, Skyler. I love you."

Skyler was lying on top of her cowboy, who was catching a nap after their second round of lovemaking. Her body couldn't seem to get enough; in fact, instead of her passion waning, it was building. She had a fire in her that Hunter had deliberately lit, and as far as she could figure, it was up to him to put it out.

She kissed his smooth, defined chest, encircling his nipple with her tongue, and used his hard thigh to ease some of the ache she was feeling.

"Why aren't you sleeping?" He mumbled the question.

"Just one more time." She reached between them and wrapped her fingers around him. He was soft now, but she was well aware of how quickly that could change in her favor.

Hunter smiled, not opening his eyes. "Bad kitty."

She bit his nipple playfully. "One more time."

"If you can get it hard," he said, still refusing to open his eyes, "it's all yours."

It took some effort, but she had always been a goal-oriented woman. Straddling him, she reached for the drawer, pulled out a condom and handed it to him.

Sleepily, he unwrapped it, tossed the wrapper on the floor with the other two, rolled it on and smiled with his eyes closed as she slid down onto his shaft. Her hands planted on his chest, her head down in concentration, she rocked her hips, building speed, moving faster and pushing down harder, until she was panting and climaxing. Somewhere along the way, Hunter had opened his eyes to enjoy the show. The moment she started to climax, Hunter held on to her hips, moving her back and forth on his cock until she felt him stiffen beneath her. With a laugh, she collapsed on top of him, finally feeling satisfied.

He wrapped his arms around her and kissed her on the neck. "For the love of God, Skyler, go to sleep. I need at least a couple of hours of sleep before I get up."

Skyler fit herself into his side, threw her leg over his leg and rested her head on his chest. "Hunter?"

"Hmm?"

"I've always dreamed of you."

"That's nice," he mumbled and she was certain, by his response, that he hadn't been awake enough to register what she had said to him. He rolled his body toward her, tightened his grip on her and added groggily, "Me, too."

"Oh, that's terrible," Molly exclaimed. "I've been so busy with my *stuff* that I haven't called, I haven't texted. I'm so sorry. Is he okay?"

"He is truly a miracle horse." Skyler was sitting on the porch in a rocking chair with Daisy curled up on her lap. "He's been getting better, a little better, day by day."

Molly had her curls gathered up in a single pompom on top of her head, so that her pretty, heart-shaped face was highlighted. "I'm so glad, Skyler."

"Me, too."

It had been a week of working and lovemaking and basking in the love she felt for Hunter. It was a love that he seemed to very much return—not just in his words, which were important and lovely, but, more importantly, in his actions. But she still hadn't told Molly and she felt guilty about it.

"I've been kind of radio silence lately," Molly said with a little frown.

"Same," Skyler said, on the verge of talking about her summer romance with Hunter for the first time.

Skyler was about to open her mouth to confess, when Molly said, "I can't believe I've been keeping this from you."

Her eyebrows drew together and her mouth closed. "Keeping what from me?"

Molly gave a little shake of her head. "I'm in love."

"What?!" Skyler sat upright, disturbing Daisy, who complained with a meow before she repositioned herself and closed her eyes.

"I am." Molly smiled softly. "I am in love."

"Don't keep me in suspense a second longer, Molly! Who is he?"

"Chase," her best friend said. "I'm in love with Chase."

"Chase Rockwell?"

Molly nodded, her cheeks flushing prettily.

"When? How?" Skyler exclaimed. "Details! I need details!"

As it turned out, she wasn't the only one having a summer romance. While she was busy finding any excuse to be naked with Hunter, Molly was having a virtual romance of her own.

"We video-chatted one night and that one call lasted for eight hours. I've never in my life had that much to say to anyone other than you.

"We've been texting and video dating, and talking on the phone ever since, and, Skyler—" Molly's amber eyes were sparkling "—he told me that he's in love with me."

"Oh, Molly…"

"He wants to marry me."

Skyler was stunned speechless. She could only stare at her friend, who was beaming with more happiness than Skyler had ever seen before.

"He wants to marry you?" she finally asked.

Molly nodded. "He told me last night."

"How could he possibly know that after such a short time? You haven't ever been in the same state much less the same room."

"He knows." Her friend's body stiffened defensively. She lifted her chin and said, "And so do I."

"Molly." She said the name in a higher-pitched tone. "You don't even know him. How could you even consider marrying him?"

"When you know, you know," Molly said with a frown. "I just know, Skyler. You're the first person I wanted to tell. I wish you were happy for me."

Skyler was taken aback. She wasn't being supportive; she was being judgmental and that's not what Molly need from her right now.

"I'm sorry, Molly," she apologized. "I am just shocked."

"So am I," her friend acknowledged. "But I love him. I do. And I already feel like I'm going to have a fight on my hands with my family. I need at least one person in our corner."

"I'm always in your corner, Molly," she reassured her friend. "Do you guys even know how all of this is going to work? Wait a minute," Skyler exclaimed at a thought that suddenly occurred to her. "Are you moving to Montana?"

"No," Molly said. "Chase knows I just got accepted to law school here. He's going to move here."

Skyler looked past the phone to her small Montana oasis, her mind whirling with thoughts. She wanted to be insanely happy for Molly, but what she really felt was concern.

"Molly," she said after a moment of thought, "I love you and I want the best for you. I just wonder…" Skyler paused, not wanting to offend or upset her dear friend.

"We've never had to hedge our words," Molly reminded her. "Just say what you want to say."

"Could you be confusing how you feel now with how you felt when you were young?"

"Like I only think I love him now because I thought I loved him back then?"

"Yes. I think that's what I was trying to say."

"No." Molly shook her head. "I know my own heart. I know my own mind. I love him."

After a moment, Skyler knew there was only one thing she could say. "If Chase is the one for you, I'm going to be on this journey with you every step of the way. I'm going to give you the most incredible budget bachelorette party New York has ever seen!"

That made Molly laugh and her laugh broke the tension that had been an uncomfortable third wheel during the conversation. "I just want you to be happy, Molly."

"I am happy." Molly smiled brightly at her. "Skyler. I'm going to marry Chase Rockwell from *Cowboy Up!* Do you know what this means?"

Skyler shook her head, deciding to wait and tell Molly about her fling with Hunter another time. This was Molly's moment to shine.

"That psychic I saw on my trip to New Orleans who saw in the tarot cards that we are destined to marry best friends was right. I told you she was right, didn't I? You thought she was crazy and I thought she was a true clairvoyant." Molly was grinning broadly. "Prepare yourself, Skyler. Because *you*. Are. Next."

Chapter Eleven

"How do you know?" Hunter grabbed a bale of hay from the trailer and walked over to the barn at the Rocking R Ranch, Chase's small ranch that bordered Sugar Creek.

Chase followed him with a bale of his own and dropped it in front of the barn. "I just do."

"You're going to marry her?" Hunter adjusted his mask before he grabbed another bale of hay.

Hunter was doing his friend a favor by dropping off some bales of hay they had just harvested at Sugar Creek. Times were tough for Chase and money was tight. Chase would do the same for him—that much he knew.

"I'm going to marry her."

"I don't get it, man," he said. "It doesn't make sense."

"It doesn't have to make sense to anyone else but me and her," Chase said. "I saw her picture on Skyler's Instagram and I knew I wanted to talk to her. When I talked to her, I knew I wanted to see her on video. When I saw her on video, I knew I wanted to marry her. It's just that simple.

Hunter stacked his bale of hay on the bale Chase had just dropped.

"That doesn't sound simple, Chase. It sounds crazy."

"Crazy is knowing that I have met the woman of my dreams and not doing everything I can to be with her," his friend countered. "I thought I was going to marry Sarah. We had everything all planned out. Right after high school we were going to elope and start a family."

Hunter's gut twisted as memories of Sarah's sharp decline and suffering flooded his brain without his consent. He didn't want his friend to be alone—he wanted him to move on from the pain of losing his first love. But like this? It didn't sit right in Hunter's gut.

Chase took a break from the work and looked him right in the eye. "I'm going to sell the ranch, get what I can out of it. I should be able to get a decent chunk of change. I'll be able to get her a nice ring."

"You're going to sell the ranch?!" The Rockwells had been at the Rocking R for generations.

"That's right."

"Are you thinking about leaving Montana?"

"I'm not thinking about it, I'm doing it."

Hunter looked around the Rockwells' small ranch. Yes, it was showing the signs of neglect—fences were down and weeds were overtaking broken-down equipment that Chase hadn't been able to afford to fix.

"You have a life here," Hunter said with a shake of his head.

"No." His friend jerked the last bale off the trailer. "*You* have a life here. I have an existence. And I'm tired of it, man. I'm over it. My dad destroyed this place—he ran this ranch right into the ground and then had the nerve to up and die and leave me to clean up his mess." Chase had always been a man who knew his own mind, that much Hunter knew. "This place is my past—Molly is my future."

Hunter couldn't think of another thing to say; in fact, her knew that once Chase made up his mind, and spoke it aloud, it was already a done deal. Life as Hunter had always known it, with his best friend living just next door, was going to change. After they finished the job, Hunter knew he had to do right by his lifelong friend.

"If this is really what you want, you know I've

got your back. I'll hate seeing this ranch sold, but we've been friends for a long damn time."

"That's true," Chase agreed, wiping the sweat from his brow. "I really appreciate you helping me out with this hay. I'll pay you back as soon as I sell the place."

Hunter brushed aside his offer. He didn't expect to be repaid. This was what friends did for each other. "If you're really serious about selling, I'll talk to Bruce and Dad about buying your herd."

"I'm dead serious about it," Chase said without hesitation. His friend studied the ground for a moment and then said, "I was kind of counting on you to be my best man."

"I'd be honored," Hunter said, pushing aside his own wishes and focusing on his friend's apparent happiness. "You name the date and I'll be there. Heck, I'll even put on a clean pair of jeans since it's a special occasion."

Liam was working Zodiac in the round pen when Hunter returned from his trip to Chase's ranch. Skyler walked over to meet him, wondering if Chase had said anything to him about Molly.

"How's he looking?" Hunter asked about the gelding.

"Liam says he's still moving in the right direction. We seem to be past the worst of it."

"That's great news."

She nodded, falling in beside him as they headed back to the round pen.

Liam raised his chin in greeting to his brother, but kept his eyes focused on the trotting gelding.

"He's still favoring his left hind at the trot, but I don't think its lameness. I still think its how he's perceiving things," the veterinarian said.

"Will we be able to ride him?" Hunter asked his brother.

"I don't see anything that would indicate that you *couldn't* ride him. But I'd like to see him out in the pasture healing for another couple of weeks."

"I'll bring another horse down from the main barn."

Liam had the gelding slow to a walk, then stop and turn toward him. The veterinarian walked over to the horse, hooked a lead rope to the halter and then patted him on the neck affectionately. "Good for you, pops."

After they put Zodiac out in the pasture with Dream Catcher, Liam took the opportunity to stop by and tinker with the old truck he was restoring.

"How's Kate?" Hunter said, asking after Liam's wife.

Liam rummaged through his tall toolbox and found the wrench he was looking for. "She's hanging in there—her life hasn't really changed. Folks still need their horses trained and they still want to take riding lessons. She's sticking to individual lessons for now. It's Callie I'm worried about."

Callie, Hunter explained to her, was Liam's eldest daughter with Kate. Callie had been born with Down syndrome, but even with an intellectual disability, she was a very accomplished young woman. Callie loved to cook and had a website and blog centered on her passion for creating home-cooked meals. She had lived in a group home in town to gain independence, had been earning her own money working at Strides of Strength equestrian program for differently abled children and was engaged to be married.

"She's upset that the wedding had to be postponed."

"Upset is an understatement." Liam frowned. "She's regressed a bit, having meltdowns and threatening to call of the wedding off entirely. I keep trying to reassure her that the wedding will happen—the country just needs to get past this rough patch."

Skyler was standing a distance away from Liam, watching as he worked on the engine.

"Does she run?" she asked, admiring the 1950s model truck.

Liam threw the wrench back into the toolbox and wiped his hands on a nearby rag. "She did. But she's being moody."

"Typical woman," Hunter joked with a wink in her direction.

"Ha, ha." She rolled her eyes at him. "Very funny."

To Liam she asked, "Do you mind if I take a look?"

Liam appeared confused about the question; he stopped wiping his hand on the rag and glanced between his brother and her.

"You want to take a look?" Liam asked for clarification. "Under the hood?"

She laughed at the question. "Of course, under the hood. Where else?"

Liam stepped back from the truck. "I don't mind."

She saw Liam and Hunter exchange a look, but she ignored it. She was accustomed to the response when she helped in her father's garage. Those who didn't know her always doubted her first.

Skyler pulled a stool over to the front of the truck, stepped up and looked inside the engine. While Hunter and Liam watched, their faces full of misogynistic skepticism, Skyler examined the engine clinically, just as her father had taught her to do. She methodically checked the distributor to see if there was a crack in the distributor cap. She then checked the spark-plug wire to ensure that they weren't cracked or frayed. The wires were secured to the spark plugs, as they should be.

She climbed down off the step stool and asked Liam, "I need to see if you have the right wrench for the job."

She dug through the toolbox, found the tool she was searching for, climbed back up on the stool and reached all the way to the back of the engine. She put her wrench on the bolt that held the distributor in place so she could move the distributor.

"Okay," she called out from beneath the hood. "Get behind the wheel and crank it when I tell you."

With an amused look on his face, Liam climbed behind the wheel.

"Turn it over!" Skyler called out to him.

At first the engine sputtered and clunked while she twisted the distributor, and then the engine started to run smoothly.

"I'll be damned!" Hunter's brother shouted over the loud noise of the engine. He revved the engine several times before he stepped out of the truck to look at the engine. "What did I miss?"

"Yeah," Hunter said. "How *did* you do that?"

"The timing was off." She grinned at them, enjoying their disbelief. "My father set up a crib for me in his office at the garage when I was just a newborn—my first rattle was a ring full of old keys from 1950s-era cars and trucks."

"Thank you." Liam sat back behind the wheel, shut it off and then cranked it again. The engine turned over without any sputtering or knocking.

Skyler leaned her head toward Hunter. "You say cattle is in your blood—well, mechanics is in mine."

* * *

"Hey, look!" Skyler and Hunter had just finished the barn chores. Hunter had brought down two geldings from the main barn—one for him to ride and the other, a thirty-year-old retired cow pony, to be a companion for Zodiac when they took the other two horses out to work.

"A four-leaf clover!" She pointed to a clump of cheerful, yellow flowers near the pasture fence. "It's a four-leaf clover! It's been right there in plain sight, this whole time?"

"Just be careful of the tall grass," Hunter said with his typical, slightly bossy tone.

Skyler rolled her eyes and said "yeah, yeah" in her mind. She was born careful.

Sometimes he acted like a parent watching over a precocious child and she didn't like it one bit. She was being judged on that *one* little fainting episode way back on her first day. Now she had the physical strength to match her mental strength. The whole Montana-babysitter routine was getting old.

Skyler picked her way through the brush to get-ter a closer look at the small yellow flowers. She leaned forward and sniffed the flowers. "Hmm. It smells so good."

"Sweet clover. We plant it for the livestock. Savannah makes clover honey every year."

"Oh," Skyler said, disappointed. "It's not a four-leaf clover after all."

"Look…" She held it up for Hunter to see. "Three leaves."

"You superstitious?" He was watching her, as he always did, with a slightly amused expression.

"Only a little." She tucked one of the clover flowers behind her ear.

She was about to embark on a list of reasons why she believed in lucky clovers, but was distracted by a sharp, burning sensation under her pant leg. She glanced down and realized that both of her boots and the bottom of her pant legs were covered in ants.

It took her a second to register in her brain that she was being *attacked* by the miniature insects, but another bite on her skin, which meant that they were also *under* her clothes, made her leap into action. She ran out of the tall grass, and screamed, "Ants! *Ants!*"

She stopped when she was out of the tall grass, then bent over and started to scrape all of the ants off of her boots and pants.

"Get off of me!" she yelled urgently. "Get. Off. Of. Me!"

Hunter was at her side, kneeling down with gloved hands and slapping at her pants to get the clingy, biting creatures off her without them attaching themselves to him.

"Are they off?" she asked urgently. "Are they off?"

"Turn around," he instructed, scanning her boots and her pants. "I think we got 'em all."

The commotion stopped for a moment while Skyler caught her breath. Then she felt a sting on the back of her thigh.

"Oh, crap." She started to hit her thigh with her hand, trying to smash the ant by trapping it between the denim and her skin. The little bugger, perhaps in the last throes of its life, bit her harder.

She dropped to the ground and started to tug on her boot. "I can't get it off. I can't get it off. Get it off!"

She held out her boot for Hunter to pull off. "Get my boot off."

"I'm getting it off," he told her, his voice even.

"Get my boot off!" She felt another ant bite her on her calf. "Ouch, you little bastard!"

"Did I hurt you?" Hunter threw her boot to the side and soon the second boot followed.

"No! The ant!" Skyler jumped up, clawed at the button and zipper of her jeans. Once unhooked and unzipped, she jumped up and down and pushed the jeans, which were sticking to her skin because of the sweat, and finally high-stepped out of the pants.

She turned around in a circle, craning her neck to look at her backside. "Do you see them?!"

Hunter found two more ants on her legs and removed them before they could bite.

"Any more?"

"Hold still."

"Any more?" she asked again, her skin stinging and burning where the fire ants had bitten.

"I'm looking," Hunter said, his tone less even. "Hold. Still."

Skyler stopped moving while Hunter looked her over. "I don't see any more."

"Well, that's a…" she began, just when she felt another bite. "Ow!"

"What?"

Skyler scowled, reached her hand into her panties, scratched her butt cheek several times and then pulled her fingers free of the cotton material to reveal the offending ant smashed between her two fingers.

"I got you." She flicked the insect away from her.

She was standing in her socks, underwear, tank top and cowgirl hat. Hunter looked at her and she looked back at him.

"He bit me right on the butt," she complained.

"You don't say," Hunter said drolly. "Too bad that *wasn't* a four-leaf clover, huh?"

Skyler had been lucky during her ranch experience—most of the days had been sunny with some warm breezes to break the heat. Hunter was forever complaining about the dry days turning all the pastures brown.

"Looks like you got your wish!" Skyler met Hunter at the door a week after the ant attack.

It was still dark and it felt like a monsoon had struck. When she opened the door, the heavy wind was blowing sheets of rain sideways, hard enough that they reached the front door. Hunter's raincoat was soaked with water and he was quickly making a puddle where he stood.

"It's messy out there." He raised his voice loud enough for her to hear over the wind. "Grab your slicker."

"I don't have one."

Hunter stared at her for a second. "You brought five bags."

"Two were pretty small," she muttered quickly. Then she asked, "Do you have one I can borrow."

He shrugged out of the one he was wearing. "Don't argue. Just put it on."

Skyler slipped on his bright yellow slicker made from heavy material. She had to cuff the sleeves so she would be able to use her hands. She felt terrible that he was going to get soaked in a couple of minutes, but when it came to the ranch work, and he told her not to argue, she gave him that respect.

Hunter ran to the truck and together they drove the short distance to the barn. They made quick work of the chores since she was able to match him stall for stall now.

"We'll stop by Bruce's place—he'll have some rain gear I can borrow." Hunter's clothes were damp but not soaking wet when he climbed behind the wheel.

"Maybe Savannah has something in my size?" she suggested.

"That's even better."

Savannah did have a raincoat closer to her own size and she was grateful to have it. The rain was driving down from the sky, pelting them as they tried to get their feeding chores done as quickly as possible. Skyler didn't want to admit it and didn't want to focus on it, but doing ranch chores in the rain was a complete drag. It was muddy, and sloshy; her jeans felt cold and clammy and the damp denim was rubbing across her skin in the most annoying way. It was hard to hear because the rain and wind masked their voices, so they had to yell at each other just to communicate.

Halfway through the first herd of cows, the tractor stopped running.

"What's wrong?" The hood of his rain slicker had fallen back and his black hair was slicked back away from his forehead. He was squinting at her against the rain.

"It just died!"

She tapped several times on the fuel gauge, but it was an old tractor and the fuel gauge was cracked and didn't seem to be operational. With a bad feeling in her gut, she twisted off the fuel cap and looked inside.

"It's dry as a bone in there." She delivered the bad news to Hunter at the same time she was wiping drops of rainwater that were dripping down her nose.

"No." Hunter looked in the tank. "I put diesel in yesterday."

"It's gone now."

"Damn." Hunter kicked at a nearby rock, then stood with his hands on his hips, his head down. He had pulled the hood back up and water was cascading, like a waterfall, over the hood and in front of his face.

"Damn," he said again. "I'm going to have go back and get diesel."

"Can't you call Bruce?" She ducked her head and tried to use the tractor as a shield from the wind.

"By the time he gets here, I could be there and back," he told her. "I'll be fine. I'm worried about you."

"I can make it," she insisted. "I'll just do the marine march my dad taught me and I'll be fine."

Hunter had to admit that, even in the rain, Skyler had hung in with him. She had insisted on working in the rain and she had insisted on returning back to the tractor to finish the job they had started. He also had to admit that Skyler saved the job; she was able to crack the injectors to prime the air out of the lines to get the diesel back in the cylinders so they could get the tractor to crank. She had been grumbling and low-level complaining about the rain and the mud and the slipperiness of the ground. That grumbling shifted to unvarnished frustration when they made it back to the cabin.

"I'm cold. Wet. Exhausted. Every muscle in my body hurts *still.*" Skyler stomped up the porch steps. "I'm stinky and dirty all of the time. I actually found sand in my ear." She held out her hands. "I have this black *gunk* caked under every single one of my nails."

He followed her up the steps not saying a word; he'd been raised up to know better than to interfere with a woman when she was mad as a wet hen.

"I've fallen in manure—that was fun." She pulled at the snaps on the front of her borrowed raincoat. "My blisters have had blisters. I didn't even know that was possible."

She sat down to yank off her muddy, wet boots. "I've been literally attacked by ants. I stink all of the time. Even that clinic strength deodorant I bought the other day has failed. Sometimes I'm so tired when I get home, I'm too tired to take a shower. I peel off my clothing—*peel*, mind you—and fall asleep on top of the covers just stinking to high heaven. What kind of life is this, anyway?"

She looked at him as if to prompt him to partici-pate in her seemingly one-sided conversation. But he wasn't much in the mood to coddle her; in fact, he was pretty ticked off at how she had managed to spin his world right off its axis.

"Suck it up, cupcake," Hunter said.

Skyler stared at him in disbelief before her eyebrows drew together; her lavender eyes turned a stormy amethyst. She stood up.

"'Suck it up, cupcake'?" she repeated as if she hadn't heard him correctly. "Is that what you said?"

"This is the life." He crossed his arms over his chest. "This is what you wanted."

"Clearly delusional." She walked past him, her soggy socks squishing on the wooden planks.

"This is the life," he repeated.

She stopped, spun around. "I *know*! Don't you think I know that by now? And I hate it! I. Hate. It! *Reality* does *not* live up to the dream—"

"It never does…"

"It's hotter, wetter, muddier, more stinky and more buggy." She pointed her finger at him as if it was his fault that the real Montana didn't perfectly match her fantasy Montana. "*And* there weren't any rabid ants in my dreams!"

Chapter Twelve

They had never quarreled before but Skyler supposed there was a first time for everything. In truth, it was probably a feat that they had managed *not* to fight for as many weeks as they had been thrown together, like two strangers forced to rely on one another on *Survivor* island.

"Ready?" Hunter asked at the bottom of the porch steps. The rain had cleared up, for now, and so had the dark clouds on the cowboy's handsome face.

She could read from his body language that he wasn't sure which version of Skyler he was going to encounter when she walked out the door to greet him.

She had a backpack slung over her shoulder. "Ready."

Daisy was lounging on the top porch step, enjoying the heat of the sun. She trilled when she saw Skyler, turned upside down, curled all four of her paws and gazed at her with love.

"I love you, too." Skyler bent down to pet the cat. "I left you plenty of food and water. And you can always go in the barn."

She stood up to find Hunter watching her as he seemed to like to do, his expression a bit guarded.

"Will she be okay while we're gone?"

"She'll be fine," he reassured her. "I asked Bruce to check on her when he comes to take care of the horses."

Hunter was pulling a horse trailer behind his truck. They were heading to the northernmost part of the ranch to move a herd to a new pasture. The grass was so dry from the lack of rain that the family had decided to rotate pastures early.

"Throw your gear in the back and I'll show you how to load the horses."

Skyler descended the steps quickly, threw her backpack in the bed of the truck and then walked to the barn. Hunter slowly pulled up the barn, parked and asked her to bring Dream Catcher out to the trailer.

"Just walk her straight on in, like there's nothing in the world wrong. If you're tense, she's going to think something's wrong and not want to load."

"Walk straight in?"

"Straight in and then turn around and put the guard bar down."

She looked into the trailer, rehearsed the directions in her head and walked Dream Catcher away from the trailer to get a straight shot in, then walked a line to the trailer. Dream Catcher didn't hesitate or stop; she walked right into the trailer behind her.

"Just like that." Hunter secured the rear guard behind Dream Catcher so she wouldn't back out.

"Did you see that?" Skyler put down the guard and gratefully pet the mare on the forehead. "We did it!"

Hunter walked the gelding named Tricky Dick out of the barn and got him loaded in the trailer. Tricky Dick wasn't as flashy and handsome as Zodiac; he was dark brown with some bleached spots on his coat from the sun and his mane and tail were black and scruffy. Hunter had said, "He's not much to look at, but he's one of the best cow ponies Sugar Creek has ever seen."

"What's in here?" Skyler pointed to the door behind her.

"That's the camper."

She raised her eyebrows with a question.

He opened the door and Skyler was hit with a blast of hot, stale air. Inside, it looked like a mini RV—there was a bed up on a platform, a small kitchenette, a bathroom and a small two-seater dining table.

"I bought this rig from my brother Gabe when he upgraded. Chase and I used to take this on the rodeo circuit."

Hunter shut the door behind them. "This rig's seen some things."

"I bet." She took his offered hand and hopped down to the ground. "Do you guys plan to do any more rodeos together?"

"Naw." Hunter frowned. "I'm pretty sure Chase's rodeo days are over."

Skyler took her spot in the cowboy's truck, certain from his last comment that he was well aware of Chase and Molly's whirlwind courtship. She knew and he knew. And yet neither one of them had wanted to say a word about it.

The ride to the northern corner of the ranch was a winding, at times bumpy, trek. For Skyler, the trip was an opportunity for them to move past the dustup that had happened between them on the porch. She was a let's-move-forward kind of woman and, luckily, it seemed that Hunter was of a like mind.

"This is a beautiful ride," Skyler sighed, feeling some of the tension of the morning drain out of her body as she breathed the fresh air deeply into her lungs.

A small half smile, one that she had grown to love even more than she had loved it on the reality TV show, appeared on his face, but he kept his eyes on the road. The trailer was heavy with the extra weight of the horses, and Hunter had already let her know that there were several spots on the back ranch road that could be challenging.

She breathed in deeply again and exhaled slowly, leaning her head back and letting the breeze from the open window and the sun filtering through the trees warm her skin. She felt disconnected from the morning when everything seemed so daunting. Now she felt content and relaxed, loving the scenery and peacefulness unfolding all around.

Hunter switched to four-wheel drive, took the rig across a narrow, shallow creek and then around a corner to a clearing. Skyler inhaled again—her breath was taken by the majesty of the mountain. It was closer than she had ever been. Up until now, these glorious peaks had been far off in the distance; now, the mountain was directly before her. She swallowed hard, several times, as she was overwhelmed by the sight before her. *This* was the Montana she had thought about for so many years. This was it. And, to be here, experiencing it with Hunter Brand, was beyond a reward for all of the months she fought so hard to survive.

"This is still Sugar Creek?" she asked, in awe.

"Brand land."

"Incredible." She pushed open the door and stepped out.

Skyler helped Hunter set up the small traveling

corral for the horses beneath a shade tree that would give them some shade and shelter. Hunter had loaded the trailer with water for the horses, but they were also close enough to a stream should their stock run out. The camper part of the trailer had been outfitted with solar panels and had a generator to run the appliances, lights, climate control and, most importantly to Skyler, the water heater.

"It's really nice in here." She sat down at one of the bench seats at the dinette. "I've seen apartments in the city about this size."

"I thought you'd prefer this to camping."

She didn't want to say that he was correct, but he was correct. Sleeping on the ground, as she discovered when she had fallen asleep the night of their first date, was not her *thing*.

"You can decide sleeping arrangements," Hunter said, taking off his hat and hanging it on a hook just inside the door.

Skyler stood up; she didn't like the distance her outburst had caused between them. She only had a finite amount of time with her dream cowboy. And even though ranch life had not lived up to the fantasy... Hunter had. He was strong, handsome, sexy and funny. He was a gentleman. A cowboy.

"I would be lonely without you in bed with me." She slipped her arms around his waist and rested her head, as she liked to do, on the part of his chest that housed his heart.

Wordlessly, Hunter wrapped his arms around her shoulders, hugged her and pressed a gentle kiss on the top of her head. He let out his breath and that was when she realized that he had been holding it.

"I'm sorry about…earlier," she said, not lifting her head. This was one of those moments she wanted to savor, burn in the memory bank of her mind and hold on to for the rest of her life.

"I'm sorry." He rested his chin lightly on the crown on her head.

"Our first fight?"

"Bound to happen."

"But we're moving forward."

"That's what I want."

She felt him give a little nod in agreement. After a moment, she lifted her head so she could see his eyes.

"I don't really hate it here."

"I know you don't. You're overwhelmed by reality here."

The fact that Hunter understood her made it easier for her to move past her embarrassment over her mini breakdown. Yes, she was overwhelmed by the daunting reality of ranch life. She was also disappointed. Her Montana experience had been a jumble of incredible highs and muddy, smelly lows. It had been a shock to have her much-loved image of Montana life shredded and patched back together to create a more realistic picture.

Hunter titled up her chin and kissed her gently on the lips. She closed her eyes and melted in his arms, savoring the warm, comfortable, safe feeling of being in the cowboy's arms.

"We'd better finish setting up camp," he murmured into her neck.

It would be too easy for both of them to get lost in each other's arms. It would be too easy to slip out of their clothes and slip into the nearby bed.

"Something to look forward to?" she asked with a small, intimate smile on her well-kissed lips.

Hunter seemed, like her, to need just one more kiss. It was a down payment, a promise, of the love-making to come. No one had ever made her feel so desirable, so sexy, so womanly. In the cowboy's arms, she had found a part of herself she hadn't know existed.

Suddenly, Hunter swung her into his arms and walked them both toward the bed.

With a laugh, she hung on to his neck. "We have work to do, remember?"

"It'll wait," Hunter said with that deep growl in his voice that made her feel excited with anticipation of the pleasure to come. "This can't."

The horses, in shadow, were busy eating their hay in the nearby corral. Hunter had given Skyler the choice of cooking in the trailer or building a fire. Skyler chose the fire. She enjoyed watching Hunter in his element—he was manly and capable and that reminded her of her father. Her father was a man's man; Chester wasn't a cowboy and he had never ridden a horse, but he was a United States Marine and a diesel mechanic. He was blue collar and showered after work, not before. Her father had always made her feel safe and cared for—that was the same feeling she had when she was with Hunter.

They were the only people for miles, sitting together at the edge of the fire, with glittering stars, bright and plentiful, strewn across the expansive blue-black sky. The day had ended on a warm note and the warmth lingered in the air, but was slowly being overtaken by a cool breeze coming from the mountains.

"This is what I will miss." Skyler was leaning back against Hunter, her face tilted up to the sky. "You can't see the stars like this back home."

She felt Hunter's arm tense around her. "I'd better check on the horses."

They had just fed them and watered them, and Skyler had the distinct feeling that Hunter needed to put some distance between them.

"Okay," she said quietly.

Their relationship had been like fireworks on the Fourth of July—a sudden burst of sparkling lights in the night sky. But, like fireworks, their relationship was, in her mind and perhaps in Hunter's, destined to be explosive, brilliant and over way too fast.

Hunter returned and stopped next to where she was still sitting by the fire, her knees tucked up to her body, her arms hugging her legs tightly. The cowboy held his hand out to her. "We'd better get some rest. Big day tomorrow."

Skyler put her hand in his—would any other hand ever feel so comfortable to hold? Could she really go home and carry this love in her heart for the rest of her life? Their relationship was still so new, still so fresh, that it didn't seem reasonable to dwell on the end of summer. They had right now and that had to be enough.

And yet there was a voice inside her brain, a voice that couldn't be silenced. She didn't believe, deep down, that she would ever have enough of the cowboy. Could she see herself leaving the city—leaving her friends, her father—and forever exchanging people for trees? She had always believed that she was a ranch girl trapped in a city girl's body. This trip had proven that false. She was a city girl. As much as she loved the endless sky and the fresh air and the babbling, clear streams, it was difficult to appreciate the glory of the landscape when she was wading through cow manure or feeding a herd of horses hours before dawn in a torrential rainstorm.

Hunter had agreed with her let's-take-it-one-day-at-a-time strategy; he hadn't discussed after the summer was over. If he asked her to stay, if he asked her to make Montana a more permanent way of life, what would she say? Was the cowboy worth giving up everything she realized she loved so much about her life in New York?

Yes. The answer was yes. Could she make Montana her home if that home included Hunter?

"Yes," she said aloud even though she meant to only say it in her mind.

"What was that?" Hunter asked, half-asleep next to her.

"Nothing." She curled up on her side and scooted back so she was tucked into the curve of his body. "Good night."

Hunter mumbled something, sneaked his arm around her and pulled her more tightly into his body, like he was holding on to a stuffed animal.

"I love you, Hunter."

"I love you."

The next morning, Hunter let her sleep just past dawn and awakened her with a campfire breakfast.

"How'd you sleep?" He handed her a cup of coffee.

"Actually, not too bad." Once her mind had finally settled down, her body soon followed.

She finished her breakfast quickly; Hunter was already saddling the horses and getting ready for them to ride out to the herd. They had practiced herding cattle several times during her time in Montana, and Skyler was feeling confident in her ability

when she mounted Dream Catcher. The most important thing she had learned was when Dream Catcher
started to keep a cow from straying, tapping into her
natural instinct as a quarter horse, tacking right and
then left, Skyler just held on to the saddle horn for
dear life and let the horse do her job.

They rode out together as the sun was rising over
the mountain peaks. They were lucky—it was slated
to be a clear day. They reached the herd positioned
near the base of the mountain. Many were lying
down while others walked slowly, grazing as they
moved, their tails waving back and forth like windshield wipers to shoo away the flies. It was going
to be tricky to move the cattle through the lightly
wooded area to the pasture that was more plentiful
with grass and foliage. There were trees and boul-
ders to avoid and Skyler would have to not let her
mind be distracted for thinking of pictures she could
capture to show everyone back home this latest leg
of her journey out west.

They both took their positions and began to move
the cattle to the east. Down a small hill, they followed an overgrown path toward the destination.
They carefully crossed the creek, wider here and
more rocky, then let the horses and cows break to
drink. A horsefly was trailing her, trying to land on
Dream Catcher's rump. Skyler spun around, waved
her hand at the large black flying insect, trying to
stop it from landing on her horse.

"Let it land." Hunter rode up beside her.

She stopped waving her arms and let the horsefly land. Hunter waited until the horsefly latched on to Dream Catcher's rump and then he slammed his hand down on the bug, killed it and then flicked it with his finger.

"Thank you," she said, taking note of how to kill the nuisance insects. Next time she would take care of it.

Hunter tipped his hat to her, his focus centered on the herd. It was a slow, often monotonous process, moving the herd. But there was also something very poetic and romantic about riding through the woods on horseback, just the two of them, with the sound of intermittent mooing mingled with the chirping of birds in the trees overhead.

"There's a calf breaking from the herd." Hunter pointed to right.

Skyler nodded. She had been trained on this and she was confident that, with Dream Catcher's skill and her ability to hold on, they could get the wayward calf back in line with the herd.

She trotted over to where the calf was curiously sniffing around a nearby tree and then Skyler saw that the calf had found some wild clover to sample. Skyler blocked the calf, whistled and waved her hat so the calf would be persuaded to abandon the clover and head back to the herd.

"Come on, little one," Skyler called out to the

calf that was determined to get one more clover before heading back.

The calf suddenly spun around, heading in the wrong direction away from the herd. Dream Catcher naturally, instinctively, blocked the calf and lowered down, moving to the left. Skyler hung on, remembering to relax her body, not stiffen it against the feeling of just being along for the ride. This was what Dream Catcher had been trained all of her life to do.

The calf turned around and jogged back in the direction of the herd. Skyler patted the mare on the neck. "Good girl."

"Nice work," Hunter said to her when she returned to her position at the back of the herd.

"All the praise has to go to Dream Catcher," she said, but she did feel proud.

Skyler settled into the saddle, letting her hips rock with the motion of the horse, keeping a watchful eye on the herd, focusing on the job, following Hunter's example. They were an hour into the job when Hunter pointed to a small incline.

"It's going to get pretty narrow up ahead."

She nodded.

"How much farther?" Skyler called out to him.

"Just on the other side of that ridge."

Her butt was starting to feel numb and she needed to relieve herself. She had learned early on in her trip that learning how to tinkle in the woods was a necessity and that public restrooms were, in fact, a luxury she had never truly appreciated.

"Just on the other side of the ridge" took another thirty minutes with the slow-moving herd meandering through the trees. As promised, there was an open field past the ridge where the herd stopped to graze.

"This is it?" she asked.

He nodded. "We can head back."

"I'm going to make a pit stop," Skyler said, and after she knew that he heard her, she trotted Dream Catcher back over to the woods.

Like a pro, she got her business done quickly and was back in the saddle in record time. She spotted Hunter up ahead, waiting for her while Tricky Dick nibbled at some leaves on a nearby tree. Skyler closed her legs and asked Dream Catcher to canter; she loved to canter.

Skyler was smiling broadly, sitting in the saddle, directing Dream Catcher, feeling like a real, authentic cowgirl. She had really grown in her time in Montana—in fact, she felt pretty certain that she could ride out her own without Hunter and feel perfectly safe.

Hunter turned Tricky Dick to face them—no doubt he'd heard the sound of hooves approaching. She caught his eye and smiled broadly, imagining how impressed Hunter must be with her riding skills, when she misjudged the height of a tree limb. She had to duck forward, wrap her arms around Dream Catcher's neck, in order to avoid being scraped off the horse's back. Just beyond the tree limb, Skyler sat upright, accidentally pulled back on the reigns, and Dream Catcher did what she was trained to do—she stopped.

Skyler fell forward, once again wrapped her arms around the horse's neck, screamed as she lost her balance, and fell out of the saddle. The horse stood stock while she dangled precariously, her arms wrapped around Dream Catcher's neck. She felt for the ground with her feet, relieved and a little shocked that she hadn't fallen.

"Thank you, Dream," she said, letting go of her grip on the horse's neck.

As she stepped backward, her heel caught on a jagged rock and she fell down.

"Owww!" She winced.

Hunter had galloped to where she was sitting. He dismounted quickly and was at her side.

"Are you okay?" he asked. "What hurts?"

"My butt." She winced, rubbing her backside.

"Anything feel broken?"

"My butt," Skyler said, irritated.

She didn't cry, but she wanted to cry. This moment was a metaphor for her trip to the Big Sky state.

"Do you think you can stand?" he asked, sticking by her side.

She nodded, holding on to his arm. She was going to be stiff, that was for sure, but she could tell that nothing was broken.

"I'm okay." She let go of his arm.

"Will you be able to ride?"

She nodded her head again, biting her lip and hobbling forward.

"You're a real cowgirl now," Hunter said as he adjusted his stride to keep pace next to her.

She winced as she leaned down to pick up Dream Catcher's reins, which had fallen over her neck when she lowered her head to graze and were now lying on the ground.

"How do you figure?"

"Sure you fell off. But you're gonna get right back on. Can't get more cowgirl than that."

—

Chapter Thirteen

He didn't want to be too obvious or appear to be hovering, because he knew that Skyler didn't like that, but Hunter kept a close watch on her as they headed back to camp. That was a fall that could ruin a person's life. She was lucky—no, *they* were lucky—that she had walked away with a bruised backside and a hurt ego. It could have been a heck of a lot worse.

Hunter knew from experience that the best thing for a fall like that, as long as there weren't any signs of severe trauma, was for Skyler to keep moving—do little jobs to keep herself from stiffening up. She was going to be sore, no doubt about that. But her body would do better if she didn't baby it too much.

After they took care of the horses, Hunter gave her some ibuprofen for the aches and pains to come and then had her jump into a hot shower while he fixed them some lunch. He knew Skyler felt bothered by her fall; he had learned her expressions and her behavior quicker than any other person he'd known in his life. Perhaps he had just paid closer attention to Skyler than he had others.

"How are you feeling now?" he asked when she emerged from the tiny bathroom, her short pixie hair slicked back from her lovely face.

"Better." She sent him a small smile.

She took a seat at the table and waited for him to join her.

"Hope you don't mind grilled cheese," he said, putting a plate down in front of her. "Not much room to bring anything fancy."

"I've never needed fancy," she said, picking up a half of the sandwich he had made for her.

He'd been thinking a lot about what Skyler might need in her life. And if he was honest with himself, he still hadn't figured it out. When he started this romance with her, he hadn't been thinking too far in the future. It was new and exciting and he acted with his heart, not with his head. But, as summer's end approached, he began to realize just how deep in it he was with Skyler.

"You know…" he said after he finished one half of his sandwich. "When I was a kid, I was all dressed up in my new cowboy boots. My new hat. I had on this gun belt with two plastic sharp shooters. I thought I was John Wayne from those old Westerns my father used to watch."

He made her smile with that image of him as a young boy and that let him know that he was on the right track telling her this story.

"My father had gotten me a pony—her name was Goldie. Now, Goldie lived up to the reputation for ponies—she was mean and ornery and didn't take too kindly to being ridden. Jock did that on purpose, because he wanted me to get a challenge right off the bat. My first ride on Goldie, I got on just fine, I got started just fine, but when I went to canter, she decided that was enough of me. She darted to the side, caught me off guard and I fell off."

"You did?" Skyler said in between bites.

He nodded with a smile at the memory. "But I didn't fall off clean like you did. My new boot got caught in the stirrup and she dragged me through a bunch of buckthorn. Man, did that hurt."

He continued while she listened attentively. Hunter wanted her to feel better and his story seemed to be doing the trick. "Goldie finally—and I would say deliberately—scraped me off on a tree."

Skyler smiled. "That's terrible. I don't know why I feel like laughing about it."

"Because it's frickin' hilarious." He laughed.

"But, man, did I hate Goldie for a second or two after that."

"But you became friends?"

Skyler had a tender heart for all living things; it was something that he genuinely appreciated about her.

"Yes. We became friends."

"That's good." Skyler's eyes had a little bit of that sparkle back in them when she looked down at her empty plate. "Is there enough for another?"

After lunch, Hunter helped Skyler stretch her muscles, putting her through the same exercises and stretches he did personally whenever he got bucked off a bull. It wasn't going to fix everything that was heading her way over the next couple of days, but it would go a long way to soften the blow.

"When are we going back?" she asked after they stepped out of the trailer.

"I asked Bruce to take care of our workload until tomorrow."

Skyler squinted against the sun, her eyes turned toward the mountain. "I want to go up to that peak. Do you know a way up there?"

"You want to ride up there now?"

"When am I ever going to get another chance?" she asked.

He picked up a twig from the ground, snapped

it between his fingers and tossed it away from him. "It's up to you. Are you sure you're up to it?"

"You said that exercise is good for me and sitting around babying myself will make things worse."

"I did say that."

She turned back to him, her lavender-blue eyes pulling him in and captivating his attention, as they always seemed to do.

"Do you know a way?" she asked.

Hunter always felt compelled to make Skyler's wishes come true. If she wanted to get up to that peak, then he was going to find a way to get there as safely as humanly possible.

He winked at her. "There's always a way."

They packed some supplies and tacked up the horses. This was familiar territory to him and he had ridden to the peak many times. In fact, in his youth, this was one of the spots Chase, Dustin and he would go to drink beer until they were almost too drunk to ride. He didn't miss the hangovers, but he did miss the close friendship he had with Chase and Dustin back when they were all together filming *Cowboy Up!*

Hunter took it nice and slow, picking each path forward carefully with Skyler in mind. It didn't surprise him that she wanted to get back in the saddle and go to the peak. In fact, he had figured out pretty quickly that Skyler was one of the most single-minded, goal-oriented, determined women he'd ever met. He had let her petite, almost fragile appearance fool him in the beginning. He had learned not to underestimate Skyler Sinclair after spending some concentrated time with her.

"We'll tie off the horses here." Hunter found a safer place for them to stop and dismount. "It's too rocky for the horses to go up to the peak."

He was at her side when she dismounted, guiding her down. When she needed help, she was the type of woman who would accept the help, another character trait he found admirable.

"You take the lead," he told her, wanting to stay behind her and catch her if she lost her footing. "Just follow this little path right up past that boulder."

Slowly, and more stiffly than she would have moved before the fall, Skyler hiked the short distance to the peak. He knew the moment when her view became unobstructed because she breathed in and then gasped with pleasure. It was a moment like this—a moment when she was surprised and delighted by her discovery—that he enjoyed the most. It was, he believed, what he would remember most fondly about his time with Skyler.

"Oh, wow." She took out her phone and began to take pictures of the expansive view from the top of the mountain. "Just look at this!"

Hunter stood back and watched her. It pleased him to see her happy. She turned her head to look back at him, to see what he was doing.

"Come here and look at this view!"

"I'm enjoying the view I have right now." He smiled at her. Whenever he complimented her, she would smile a bit shyly at him, her eyes shining, a pretty blush staining her cheeks.

She finished grabbing the images she wanted to add to her story, put her phone away and then carefully walked over to where he was standing, took his hand and led him back over to where she had been standing.

"I want to share this moment with you," she said honestly.

Hunter found that he just couldn't deny her anything. He stood behind her, wrapped his arms around her and held on to her. She leaned back into his body with a happy sigh and held on to his forearms so they were completely connected.

"I love you," she said simply.

It was so soft, so quiet, the words being swept away from him on a quick gust of wind, that he almost thought he had imagined it.

He turned her gently in his arms; he wanted to look down at her face.

"And I love you." He tilted her chin up and kissed her on that mountain peak. It occurred to him that she was the first woman he had ever kissed here and he was glad for it. He wanted this moment to be special—a moment just for them. He kissed her again, knowing that he would never stop wanting to share kisses with this woman. And yet he couldn't seem to take the leap that Chase had taken. Chase could see himself in the city with Molly; no matter how hard he tried, Hunter couldn't see Skyler living full-time out west. And he knew, without any doubt, that he could not make his life in New York. Sugar Creek was his lifeblood; he was bound to this land and could not leave it.

They had packed a snack so they could sit at the top of the mountain and enjoy the view for a while. Together, they found a flat spot on the mountain face and sat down. Skyler said her tailbone still ached and that she had a feeling that she was going to sport a serious couple of bruises, but she had been in pain before—she had suffered before. The discomfort she was feeling now paled in comparison to the enjoyment she was having and he was glad to hear it.

After she finished her snack, she stood up, allowing him to give her a hand, and then walked over to the edge of the peak.

"Careful." Hunter was right on schedule with his warning.

"I will be," she promised.

Hunter was protective by nature, but Skyler, in particular, he felt the need to protect. Not only because she was an accident-prone neophyte, but also because he loved her so damn much.

She stood with her arms open wide, held back

her head and shouted as loudly as she could, "I'm on top of the world!"

She turned around and smiled broadly at him. "Look at me, Hunter! I'm on top of the world!"

"I see you."

This Skyler was entirely different from the woman whom he had met in the airport at the beginning of summer. She had put on weight—she had built muscle naturally from lifting bales of hay, mucking stalls and riding horseback. She was still petite but built more like a gymnast at the height of their training. Her hair had grown back shaggy and messy and she was always pushing at it, but he liked how wild and crazy it was. She reminded him of a wood nymph in a fairy tale, mischievous and full of life. Her skin, once a gray, pasty hue, had turned golden with a rosy undertone. Standing with her hands on her hips, a sweet, shy sparkle in her eye, her feet planted apart with a small smile on her face, Hunter knew that he had never seen a more beautiful woman in his life.

Skyler continued to smile at him, and when he didn't say anything, just kept right on looking at her, she dropped her arms and asked, "What?"

"What?" He was snapped out of his own thinking by her question.

"Why are you looking at me like that?"

"I think you're beautiful. Can't I admire you?"

"If you must," she said with a flirty, sassy tone she was just beginning to use with him. She came over to where he was sitting and made a noise that let him know she had felt some pain when she bent down, which made her laugh at herself before she kissed him playfully. "I hope you don't mind if I admire you, too, cowboy."

That night, Hunter had an odd feeling in his gut. He wanted to savor every moment of their lovemaking, really take his time, memorize the gentle curve of her hip, how soft her skin felt in contrast to the roughness of his own. He loved the firm pertness of her breasts; he loved to suckle those pert nipples until Skyler was panting and digging her fingernails into his arm. He loved the scent of her, the taste of her.

Hunter kissed her between her thighs, lingered there to ready her body to take him in. Then he kissed a trail across her flat stomach and dropped one last kiss on the small, round, puckered scar where the chemo port had brought her life-saving medicine that had saved her and allowed her to come into his life. It had crossed his mind more often than he liked that he could have been robbed of ever having known this incredible woman at all.

"I don't want to hurt you." Hunter was on his side.

"I think it will be better if I'm on top," she agreed.

Hunter rolled onto his back, rolled on a condom and held his arms out for Skyler. Her legs on either side of his body, she sank down on him and they both moaned in unison. He hugged her to him, body-to-body, skin-to-skin, rocking gently together as he covered them with the blanket. He wanted to wrap them up in a cocoon and shut out the world completely. He closed his eyes, focused on the feelings of being enveloped by her warmth, the tightness of her body, how incredible it felt to be inside her, pleasing her as he pleased himself.

It was quiet, her first orgasm. She held on to him, her head tucked into his neck, his hands on her back. He was careful not to run his hands over her backside, as he loved to do. The noises she made as he brought her to climax made him want to join her, but he forced himself to hold off. He didn't want this to end.

"Yes, my love." He held her tightly while she shuddered in his arms.

She was still for a moment, catching her breath. Then she kissed his chest and pushed herself upright. She wanted more of him; she always wanted more. And he knew, more than ever before, that this was the first time in his life that a woman was truly *making love* to him, with him. Skyler was loving him with her body, showing him with every kiss, every moan, every time she caught his gaze and let him see her in her moment of climax, that it was an act of love.

The blanket slipped down her back as she lifted her hands to put them flat on the low roof above the bed. Her breasts white and round, her nipples looking like small rosebuds, she bore down on his shaft, taking him in as deeply as she could and rocking her hips while her strong thighs anchored her to him. He put his hands on her hips and watched his love take her pleasure. Just before she reached another crest, she fell forward into his arms, whispered "I love you" in his ear, and they both rode a glorious wave together. Hunter dropped kiss after loving kiss on her face, on her lips, on her chin, on her cheek.

"You are my first love." Hunter wanted her to know this. He wanted her to carry this knowledge with her always, no matter what happened. "My very first love."

That night, by the campfire, Skyler felt a particular form of contentedness. Yes, her body ached, but her heart was full of love for the cowboy. They loved each other—that was undeniable now. The question remained: What would they ultimately do about it?

"This place seems familiar to me. I can't put my finger on it."

Hunter stoked the fire for a moment before he said, "We filmed *Cowboy Up!* here for several episodes."

Skyler sat up with the realization. "That's it! That's why it seems so familiar."

"We used this same firepit," he added.

She loved the fact that she was sitting at one of

the locations of the show. She didn't express her feelings, sensitive to Hunter's dislike of his history with the show.

Hunter sat back on his haunches, staring into the fire, lost in his own thoughts. After a moment, he chuckled to himself and then sat back on the ground.

"What?"

"I was just thinking back to something that happened during filming one season," Hunter said with another laugh. "I went off into the woods to relieve myself—I went pretty far out in the woods because we had the film crew with us and I don't know…" He shrugged. "I didn't really trust them—they were from LA."

"City folk can be suspicious," she interjected teasingly.

He smiled as he continued. "I was just about done and I look down and realize that I had been relieving myself on a snake."

Skyler wasn't expecting him to say that. "Oh, no!" She laughed, surprised.

"I jumped back like I had been bitten for real," he said. "I didn't have to pee anymore, I can tell you that. The snake was about four feet long, impressively thick…"

"Venomous?"

He nodded. "I had taken a whiz on a prairie rattlesnake."

"Was it asleep? Why didn't it move?"

"I was wondering the same thing," he said. "So I found a sharp stick and poked it. Probably not the smartest idea, but that's what I did. It was dead, so I stabbed it with the stick and carried it back to camp. Told everyone that I killed it."

Skyler laughed along with him, enjoying this storytelling side of Hunter.

"Hey…wait. I remember that episode. They filmed you with that snake."

He nodded, his smile dropping just a bit. Then he flashed her a self-effacing half smile. "I never did tell them that I found it dead. You're the only one who knows that secret."

She crossed her heart with her finger. "I'll never tell."

After a minute, Hunter added, "You know, the first thing that I thought when I saw that I was peeing on a snake?"

"What?"

"That if I got bit by a venomous snake on the head of my *snake,* as it were—" he grinned at her with good humor "—there wouldn't be anyone back at camp who would be willing to suck the venom out."

Skyler laughed so hard that her stomach hurt a bit.

"Not one of them would have taken pity on me," he told her.

"Not even Chase?" she asked, still laughing.

"Heck no," Hunter said. "He'd say 'Sorry, bro—you're dead.'"

They continued to laugh together and then Skyler asked, "Wait. Wasn't there a girl on the show? What was her name?"

Hunter stopped laughing and she regretted even bringing it up. Up until then, they had been having a great time. "Sarah."

"That's right," she said. "Sarah."

The cowboy breathed in deeply and then let it out. He stared into the fire for a good long while before he seemed ready to talk again. She could read Hunter well—as well as she could read Molly or her dad, but it had happened in a much shorter amount of time.

"You asked me once why Jock let you come here."

She nodded. She had always wondered that. It would have been so easy to cancel on her.

Hunter looked at her over the fire, his brilliant blue eyes catching the yellow and orange light from the fire. "He let you come because of Sarah."

She didn't understand and she told him as much.

"Sarah was one of my best friends—we grew up together. She was the daughter of Jock's best friend." He was staring at the fire now. "She was also Chase's girlfriend."

Skyler's stomach tensed as she anticipated something she didn't necessarily want to hear. Why would

Jock let her come to Sugar Creek because of someone named Sarah?

"Sarah wasn't there to film that show—the one with the snake—because she had just been diagnosed with cancer."

"Oh," Skyler said softly. "I see."

"Brain cancer."

"I'm so sorry, Hunter." She said it and she meant it. "I am so sorry."

He swallowed hard, lowered his head and gave her a quick nod.

"It wasn't six months later and we lost her," Hunter continued, his head still down. "We all lost Sarah. Sarah's father took it the hardest and it wasn't too long before he joined her in the grave."

Skyler put her hand over her mouth, saddened for Hunter and his family. His friends.

Hunter looked up at her then. "I believe Jock invited you here to help me."

"To help you?"

"I've never quite gotten over Sarah's death. She was my sister…" His voice had a catch in it. "Not by blood but choice."

The picture came into focus for Skyler—Hunter hadn't been able to save Sarah, but Jock believed that he could find some closure by helping her heal.

"Did it work?" she asked.

He looked up again this time with a question in his eyes.

"Did I help you?" she persisted.

Hunter stared across the fire, his eyes so intent on her face. "You've helped me more than anyone in my life, Skyler. For the first time, I feel like I can finally let Sarah rest in peace."

Chapter Fourteen

Skyler had difficulty sleeping that last night they were away from home base. Hunter slept beside her—he seemed to fall asleep so easily—while she stared up at the low ceiling, thinking. The subject of Molly and Chase's relationship had still not been broached. After the discussion about Sarah, something that seemed to be a gut-wrenching subject for Hunter, Skyler had decided to not raise the question she had regarding Chase's sudden attachment to Molly. But there were many questions on her mind.

The next morning, they had packed up the campsite and loaded the horses. Their work was done and so was their minibreak from the routine of their ranch chores.

"Time to go." Hunter got behind the wheel. He glanced over at her. "Ready?"

She had her elbow resting on the open window, taking one last look around, wanting to commit it to memory. "Ready."

Once they had crossed the stream and Skyler knew the toughest terrain was behind them, she turned her body slightly toward Hunter.

"Can I ask you something?"

"You can ask me anything you want."

"Do you know about Chase and Molly?"

He hesitated, and in that hesitation, she knew that the answer was yes. He did know.

"Yes. Chase told me."

She waited a moment to see if he would say anything else. When he didn't, she prompted, "And...?"

Hunter shook his head as if he was having his own conversation with himself. Then he said, "I don't know what to think about it, to be honest."

He glanced over at her. "What about you?"

"I think it's too fast."

"I think so, too."

"I think that they've never been in the same place at the same time."

"I said that to him."

"I said it to her." She braced her hand on the dashboard when they hit a deep bump in the rustic road.

"And?"

"She says she loves him."

"He said the same."

They were both quiet for a moment before Skyler asked, "Last night you told me about Sarah."

He nodded.

"Do you think Chase has told Molly about her?"

"I don't know."

"I don't want to offend you, Hunter, I just want to protect my friend…"

"You won't offend me."

"Do you think that Molly is some sort of rebound for him? I know it's been years, but time doesn't always heal."

"I don't think it's a rebound," Hunter insisted, but she still didn't feel reassured.

"Do you think he really loves her?"

"He sounded like it." He glanced over at her curiously. "Do you think she loves him?"

She breathed in on the thought, then exhaled and said, "Yeah. I think she does. Or at least she thinks that she does."

The conversation waned and neither of them seemed too eager to pick it back up. As they approached the settled part of the ranch, with Bruce and Savannah's small stake appearing in the far-off distance, Hunter said, perhaps as a way to button up the subject, "I hope it works out for them."

"So do I," she agreed and she meant it sincerely. Molly deserved to have a lifetime of love and she hoped that Chase turned out to be the man who could give that to her.

"We are sitting in a glass house," she openly mused.

"Meaning?"

"Maybe we don't have much of a leg to stand on, really. We jumped in pretty quick without much of an exit plan."

That brought his eyes, a bit narrowed, to her face. "Yes, we did."

There was an odd silence between them, but it wasn't comfortable, like most of their lulls in conversation were. This felt different.

"Maybe we need to fix that." Hunter's hands had tightened on the wheel, the knuckles on his hands turning white. Then he loosened his grip.

She waited, holding her breath for a second before letting it out. Did he mean "fix it" as in figure out their exit plan? Or was this the beginning of some sort of proposal?

He turned them toward Liam's cabin, his eyes steady on the ranch road. "Do you think that you could ever see yourself here...full-time?"

It was a question she had asked herself so many times and recently she had gotten to *yes*. Geography couldn't be the reason for the love she felt for Hunter to be lost—the only thing that really gave her pause was the idea of leaving her father entirely without family. He was a widower and she was his only child—the thought of leaving him alone hurt her heart.

She was formulating her response when her phone started to go crazy. She fought to fish it out of her back pocket and then looked at the screen. A slew of text messages and emails from several days ago were loading into her phone now. And there were missed calls.

"Oh, no!" Skyler read the first text message and then the next.

"What's wrong?" Hunter's phone was chiming, as well.

"My father." She was already dialing Molly. "They think he had a stroke."

Hunter felt unmoored and odd as he pulled up to Liam's cabin for what would be the last time he would come to pick up Skyler. He reflected back on the first time he had brought her to what she called her oasis in the world. He had resented her; he had wanted to be rid of her. And now all he wanted to do was hold on to her, to keep her close.

He shut off the engine and studied Skyler sitting on the front porch, her antique-wallpaper luggage stacked near the steps. Daisy was curled up in her lap. Skyler looked over at him, caught his eye, but her usual smile was not present.

"Everything set for today?" he asked when he reached the porch.

She nodded. "They couldn't get a charter on such short notice but I got a seat on a commercial flight."

The doctors had confirmed that Chester Sinclair had experienced a stroke and Skyler didn't hesitate to cut her time in Montana short.

"You'll be okay?" he asked, picking up two of her bags to load in the truck.

"I'm stronger now," she said. "I'll be okay. I have to get home to my father."

He packed up her luggage and she was still on the porch with Daisy curled up on her lap. There were tears in her eyes when she looked up from the cat. "I shouldn't have started a relationship that I couldn't finish."

It struck him that the same could be said for their relationship, and perhaps, she was saying that, too.

"How will she be okay without me?"

"I will take her to Oak Tree Hill with me," he promised. Daisy had become a part of Skyler, so naturally, she was a part of him.

"Okay," she said, hugging the cat to her chest. She kissed her on the head, then put her down next to the rocking chair. Daisy meowed loudly and gazed up at Skyler.

"She knows something's wrong," she told Hunter.

There wasn't anything he could say to make it better, so he remained silent. Skyler stood up and looked around.

"What about the horses?"

"I'll take them back up to the main barn."

"Even Zodiac?" she asked. Liam was still monitoring him and hadn't cleared him for work.

Hunter wrapped his arms around her, rested his chin on the top of her head, as he liked to do, and gave her a shoulder to lean on.

"Don't worry about the animals right now. I've got them covered. Let's just get you home to your dad."

Holding hands, Hunter escorted Skyler down the stairs to the truck.

She paused and looked back at the barn. "I wonder if I should just say one more goodbye to the horses."

"No." He coaxed her forward. "It will never be enough."

"No," she echoed, looking around, seemingly to make a mental recording of her ranch oasis. "It will never be enough."

He opened the door for her and waited for her to get in and buckle up. Then he shut the door firmly behind her. He didn't feel as strong or confident as he was showing to Skyler; she needed him to be the backbone for them both right now. Inside, he was torn in two. He hadn't expected to say goodbye so soon. Hunter hadn't had time to prepare himself; he hadn't had to time to work through their geography problem. And now she was returning home and he had no idea if their romance, so new and unexpected for both of them, would be able to survive the distance.

"Do you know, we don't have a picture of us together," she said as they pulled onto the highway, leaving Sugar Creek land.

Skyler had been very considerate about his aversion to social media. He still got a knot in his gut when he remembered what it felt like to be a teenage kid on the receiving end of so much simultaneous obsession and venom. He had been very careful about his image once the show was canceled. And Skyler, to her credit, hadn't taken pictures of him while she was photo-journaling her trip for her supports, coworkers and friends back home.

"That's my fault," he admitted.

"It's like we didn't exist at all."

"You don't really believe that," Hunter said more sharply than he had intended.

"I don't know what I believe." Skyler rubbed her hands over her face, dark circles from stress and lack of sleep noticeable beneath her eyes. "This isn't how I expected things to end between us."

He glanced over at her; he wished that he wasn't driving while they were having this conversation. He wished that it didn't feel inappropriate to discuss a heavy subject like their geographically challenged relationship when she was so worried about her father.

"This isn't goodbye," he said, and he heard the certainty resonated in his own voice.

"It isn't?" she asked doubtfully.

"Not for me." He took his hand off the wheel for a second to squeeze her hand reassuringly. "It's not goodbye—it's 'see you later.'"

That got a small smile out of her. "Okay."

At the airport, Hunter pulled in front of the terminal to unload the baggage. Before he took the truck to the parking lot, he asked the baggage handler to take a picture of them. They took off their masks and posed for the picture.

Skyler put her mask back on and took her phone from the gentleman. "Thank you."

Skyler looked at the picture and then showed it to him. "We look good together I think."

"I think so."

After she was checked in, Skyler wandered over to the carousel where he had seen her for the first time.

"I never did get a chance to go to the museum."

He turned her around and wrapped her up in his arms. "Hey. Montana will still be here. The museum will still be here. I will still be here."

They stood together for many minutes, the world going about its business while they were stuck in that one moment together. When boarding for her flight was called, Hunter tightened his hold on her.

"I love you, Skyler." He looked into her eyes so she would see that he meant it.

"I love you."

For the briefest of moments, they slipped down their masks and kissed.

"Remember," he said after he pulled his mask back up. "It's not goodbye. It's 'see you later.'"

She nodded and began to walk away from him.

"Don't forget me, Skyler," he called after her.

She turned around. "I've loved you almost all of my life, Hunter. How could I ever forget you?"

"Molly!" Skyler was relieved and grateful to see her friend awaiting her arrival. "I'm going to hug you," she said to her friend.

"I get tested every day at my new job," Molly told her. "Hug away."

They hugged each other tightly. Skyler was grateful to have Molly, the closest thing to a sibling she had in her life, to help her navigate the next several days. They managed to MacGyver her luggage into the early model Toyota Molly had borrowed from her aunt.

"I'm so sorry about your dad," Molly said as she navigated out of the parking garage and pointed them toward home.

"I still feel like I'm in shock," Skyler said while sending Hunter a text that she had landed safely.

"Of course."

"First Mom dies from complications related to COPD, and then Dad has to handle my diagnosis without her, and now he's in the hospital with a stroke? He doesn't deserve it."

"Neither do you," her friend said.

Skyler couldn't deny that it felt like the worst kind of luck, but she couldn't dwell on it. She needed to dwell on how to make her father whole.

"How does it feel to be back?" Molly asked.

"Weird," Skyler admitted. "Different worlds."

"I bet," her friend said. "You look amazing."

Skyler touched her hair. "I need a haircut. It feels really good to be able to say that again."

"Mom will do it for you. She's been cutting the neighbor's hair on the balcony. Strange times."

"If she'd be willing, I would really appreciate it. I'm starting to feel like a Muppet."

They arrived at Skyler's 1930s single-family two-story house in Queens—it had seen better days. The whitewash paint was more gray than white and the roof had needed replacing for years. Her mother had always been the iron fist when it came to maintaining curb appeal. Molly helped her drag her heavy bags up the steps to the house.

"You packed a ton." Molly lugged the last bag up to the top step.

"I didn't wear half of the stuff." She put the key in the door. "I could've taken one suitcase and a carry-on."

Once inside the front door, which opened directly into the living room, Skyler turned on the lamp just inside of the door and looked around. There were papers strewn on the floor near her father's favorite recliner chair and a bowl of half-eaten popcorn on the scratched, 1970s coffee table that her father had refused to let go.

"I wish I could stay." Molly sent her a regretful look. "I tried to get out of my shift."

Skyler hugged her friend tightly. "Thank you, Moll. I'm so lucky to have you in my life."

"Same." Molly squeezed her tight. "Keep me in the loop. I check my phone on breaks."

"I will."

"And I'll be back tomorrow."

Skyler shut the door behind her friend, locked it and then looked around with a heavy sigh. She had called her father on the way home from the airport and he sounded in good spirits, except for the fact that he was upset that she had cut her trip short. Over the course of the summer, her father had come to believe that her trip out west was exactly what she had needed to reboot her life.

"Don't come home," he had told her in a complete 180-degree reversal of his initial response to her trip.

"I'm coming home," she had said in a tone that brooked no argument. He hadn't convinced her *not* to go and now he wasn't going to convince her to stay while he was in the hospital.

Skyler moved around the two-story house in a bit of a daze, picking up papers and putting them in the recycling, gathering up random dishes and stacking them in the sink. Her father had returned to bachelor life in her absence—not completely messy, but not overly concerned about keeping a tidy house. Room by room she made her way through her childhood home, finding a shirt or a pile of grease-covered uniforms from the garage along the way. The house felt empty and sad, and she knew that she would need to keep herself busy straightening the house and unpacking her bags while she awaited her father's release.

The dishes had been washed and were drying in the dish drain; the uniforms were in the washing machine. Skyler rolled her largest piece of luggage through the house to the back door. She opened the door and was greeted with the concrete slab between the house and her garage apartment. Weeds pushed up through cracks in the slab and it was odd that this was one of the only splashes of greenery she could see.

In that moment, she missed the trees of Montana, so plentiful and fragrant, desperately. Or perhaps she just missed Hunter desperately. As if he had picked up her thoughts on some mutual wavelength that connected them, no matter how many miles separated them, Hunter called.

She quickly picked up the phone on the first ring.

"Hi."

"Hi," he said back. "I miss you."

"I miss you so much," she said, juggling the phone and the suitcase as she continued on her path toward her apartment.

"I have Daisy with me," he told her.

"Thank you, Hunter. I need her to be okay."

"She is," he reassured her. "The question is, how are you? How is your father?"

She wrestled her suitcase through the door to her apartment and then collapsed on the couch. She had, in fact, missed her couch. It was the perfect fabric and so comfy. She sat up long enough to kick off her shoes before sinking back, with a happy sigh, into her couch. They spoke for an hour with a promise to speak the next day. One by one, she got her bags into the apartment. Before Sugar Creek Ranch, she would not have had the strength to travel across country, begin to clean her father's house and still get her bags to the apartment.

But now she was tired, and all she could think about was crawling into her own bed, getting some sleep and then going to visit her father as soon as visiting hours started the next day. Thank goodness the hospitals were now allowing visitors.

A quick shower later, Skyler set the alarm on her phone, then ran her fingers over the only picture of her and Hunter together that she had set as her home screen wallpaper.

A text came through from Hunter in response to her text letting him know that she was going to sleep. Sleep well, my love.

The bed, her wonderful mattress, felt like home to her. Her pillows, her blanket, her sheets. But the bed was lonely without Hunter. She missed his body making everything too hot; she missed fighting over the blanket, each accusing the other of being a blanket hog. She missed being able to curl up next to him, put her hand over his heart and smell the wonderful scent of his skin. That night, as the sounds of her neighborhood kept her up instead of lulling her to sleep, Skyler wished she could get Scotty to beam Hunter right into her bed. No, that wasn't true. She wished that Scotty would beam her, and her bed, back to Montana. Somewhere along the way, the real Montana—the one with the rabid ants, giant horseflies, mud and manure, had begun to feel more like home than New York. She didn't know it before she left Sugar Creek…but she knew it now. Montana was Hunter's home; and for her, wherever Hunter was, that was home for her, too.

Chapter Fifteen

"I'm okay, Sky." Chester Sinclair slumped into his recliner.

Skyler watched as her father tried to use the lever to recline the chair; her father had had a stroke on the right side of his brain, which had caused some weakness on the left side of his body.

She rushed over to his chair, helped him recline and then didn't take offense when he growled at her for helping him when he didn't need it. Her father was a lefty, which made this stroke a serious blow. Yes, he had other mechanics that worked in his shop, but with the pandemic and people driving less, business had slowed and he was already struggling to make ends meet. In order to not lay off any workers, Chester had been taking in some overflow clients from a company that had some older model diesel trucks. Now he was going to have to give up that revenue stream, and if he couldn't come up with another solution, he would have to start furloughing workers.

"Dad." Skyler kneeled by his recliner, acutely aware of the fact that at the beginning of summer, and not all that long ago, he had been the one kneeling beside her chair. "It's going to be okay."

Chester put his hand on her face, looked her over real good. "You're better. That makes everything okay for me."

Skyler had a ton of ideas about how to keep them afloat while Chester was recovering, none of them her father was going to like. So she decided it would be best for her to let him settle in to the routine of physical and occupational therapy for his left-side weakness and then she would broach some touchy subjects with him.

"Here's the remote." She brought him the control for the TV. "Molly and I will be in the apartment if you need us."

"I'm glad you're home, Mr. Sinclair." Molly had her hip leaning against the kitchen counter. When she had first come to this house for a sleepover, Molly had to stand on her tiptoes to reach a plate of cookies Skyler's mom had made for them.

"Thank you, Molly." Her father always had a smile for Molly.

Skyler leaned down, gave her father a kiss on the cheek and then she and her friend walked to the back of the house toward the apartment.

"He's going to get better," Molly said, her hazel eyes concerned. "He'll get some therapy and he'll get better."

Skyler sent her friend a brief smile while she unlocked the door to her apartment. She did believe that her father was going to get better. He was strong and determined, and she had seen life knock him down plenty of times before. Chester Sinclair had always gotten back up and worked so hard that he was even better off than before.

"I have to learn how to cook," Skyler mused, looking at the pile of luggage still yet to be unpacked. "No more takeout for him. He has to be on a healthy diet."

She exchanged a look with her friend and said, "He's going to hate that."

They both laughed. Chester was a steak-and-potatoes kind of guy—getting him to change his diet and start to exercise was going to be a challenge. But if she could worm and herd cattle, she believed she was more than up for the task.

"Do you want me to help you get this done?" Molly nodded toward the luggage.

Skyler lifted her shoulders with a sigh. "No. I'm

not ready to tackle this. I actually wanted to talk to you about something."

Molly knew her well enough to know that they weren't about to discuss something frivolous. Her friend took her typical seat on the sofa and curled her legs beneath her.

"What's going on?"

Skyler joined her on the couch, sitting cross-legged and facing Molly. "I don't know why I've waited to tell you this."

Molly waited for her to finish.

"But Hunter and I…" She stopped for a moment to find the exact right words. "Fell in love."

Molly's heart-shaped face went from surprised to joyous quickly. She stood up, sat down next to Skyler and hugged her tightly.

"I'm so glad," her friend said. "I was so worried that I would have Chase and you wouldn't have your own cowboy."

Now she was glad that she waited to tell Molly. This was the kind of moment she could look back on with a smile for the rest of her life—the day she told Molly that she was in love with Hunter Brand, and now Hunter Brand was in love with her!

Molly, of course, asked the obvious question. "But why didn't you tell me sooner?"

"I don't know," she said honestly. "I think it was so new and so unreal that I couldn't bring myself to talk about it. Not even with you."

She reached out and squeezed Molly's hand. "I'm sorry."

Molly shook her head quickly, her wild curls dancing about her shoulders. "Don't you worry about it for one more second, Sky. I'm just happy. For both of us."

Her friend sat back, her face beaming. "We both got our cowboys. It really happened for us."

"Well…" Skyler wanted to temper Molly's enthusiasm. There hadn't been any promises or proposals and even plans between them. "I'm not sure there's a cut-and-dried status category for us. He has his life at Sugar Creek and I have to make sure that the bills get paid around here."

"It's going to work out for you." Her friend had always been an optimist. In fact, Molly had never faltered in her belief that she was going to survive cancer.

"You know what makes me feel happy right now, Moll?" Skyler said. "To see you so happy with Chase."

She meant it sincerely. She didn't know where her relationship with Hunter was going to go, and that was just the reality of the current moment. But to see Molly glowing from being in love with Chase was just as rewarding as if it was happening to her.

"Your cowboy is coming," Skyler said with a smile.

"Your cowboy is coming, too," her friend said emphatically. "Just you wait and see."

They talked for nearly two more hours, bouncing from one subject to another, and then Molly had to go home and get ready for work. Skyler was still on leave from the insurance agency; she had some serious thinking to do about her next steps. Unfortunately, none of those next steps would lead her back to Hunter anytime soon.

"We've been missing you at the family events." Hunter's eldest brother, Bruce, had come up to his place among the ancient oak trees. It was a rare visit to his remote and private stake on Sugar Creek.

"Is that right?" Hunter was sitting on the two-seater bench that he had carved with Daisy curled up next to him.

Bruce had grown a beard and he needed a haircut, but his ocean-blue eyes, the same as his own, were both curious and concerned. As the eldest of the siblings, Bruce was expected—by Jock—to wrangle his brothers and sister if they looked like they were straying from the herd.

"Mom is worried about you."

That was a punch to the gut; he never wanted to upset his mother. And yet that knowledge wasn't enough to make him want to break out of his self-imposed isolation. After Skyler's trip was abruptly cut short, and his life returned to the way it was before she had arrived, Hunter found that his preference to be alone now extended to his family, too.

"And Dad?" Hunter asked, knowing that news of Brandy and Dustin's relationship had burned through the gossip wires in Bozeman like a wildfire.

"Pissed off."

"That's about right." He looked down at Daisy and the cat lifted her head, gazed up at him lovingly and then meowed.

Bruce lowered himself to the ground, grunting a bit. "You need something to sit on around here."

"I don't get many visitors," Hunter countered.

"Nothing to visit, really." His brother looked around.

They didn't speak for a while; Hunter waited for Bruce to say what he was really there to say.

"You look like hell, bro," Bruce noted.

Hunter reached up and scratched his scruffy facial hair. He could use a shave. And he could put on some clean clothes.

When he didn't add to the conversation as he knew Bruce expected him to, his brother said, "Everybody—Mom, Dad, me—thinks you got involved with the woman from New York."

"Her name is Skyler."

Bruce knew right then—Hunter could read it in his face—that the family's suspicion about the nature of his relationship with Skyler was true.

"So it's true." His brother had a grim expression on his face. "What about Brandy?"

Hunter stood up, frustrated, disturbing Daisy. The cat got up, executed a Halloween-cat stretch and then turned around in a circle several times before she curled back up on the bench.

"Brandy doesn't want anything to do with me and the feeling is mutual. She was a pain in the butt when we were kids and the only thing that's changed now that's she's older is that she's a heck of a lot prettier than she used to be. But still a royal pain in the ass."

Hunter paced a little beside the firepit. "And the fact that Jock got his hopes up that I was going to marry Brandy and then have a grandchild that would tie the two ranches together was nuts!"

He stopped pacing. "You see that that was nuts, right?"

"You and Brandy could've hit it off," his brother said.

"Well, we *didn't*."

Bruce held up his hands. "Okay. So you didn't. That still doesn't explain why you've been living like a hermit out here with that cat."

"I'm figuring things out."

"Like what?"

"Like," Hunter said pointedly, "how I'm going to get Skyler back home where she belongs."

* * *

The visit from his brother did have the benefit of "snapping him out of it." After Bruce left, Hunter got himself cleaned up. He shaved, put on clean clothes and headed over to Chase's ranch. Chase was the person in his life, a brother from another mother, who would understand his dilemma with Skyler.

When he pulled onto the neglected driveway to the Rocking R Ranch, Chase was near the fence putting up a For Sale by Owner sign. Hunter got out of his truck and walked over to his friend.

"This makes it real," he said.

"Yeah." Chase had been hand-digging a hole for the wooden signpost. "It's real. Molly told her folks about us last night."

Hunter helped Chase lift up the heavy signpost and together they put it into the hole.

"Oh, yeah? How'd that go?"

They both pushed dirt into the hole, helping the signpost to be more secure. Then Chase used the shovel to tamp down the loose dirt.

"Not too bad, considering." Chase leaned on the shovel for a moment. "I think they were hoping for a more of a white-collar kind of guy for Molly."

Hunter nodded his understanding. A lot of parents had a certain idea of who they wanted their adult children to marry—he was living proof of that.

"Six years in the army did help soften the blow

for them." Chase threw the shovel in the back of Hunter's truck.

After the show got canceled, Chase had joined the army. He might have gone far in the armed forces if his parents hadn't desperately needed his help on the ranch. Chase's father had been a great guy, but he was lousy with money. When they were growing up, everyone knew that the Rockwells were always on the brink of financial disaster. All of Chase's money from the show had gone to his family and even that hadn't been enough to save them.

Hunter drove them to the house. The Rockwell house had been built in the 1920s—it was a small two-story house with whitewashed boards and a rusty tin roof. There was a front porch with an old swing where Linda Rockwell, Chase's mother, had treated Hunter with homemade root beer.

As he parked, he stared at the house, memories of his childhood—great memories—rushing over him.

"We had some good times here, didn't we?"

"We did," Chase agreed. His friend didn't say it, but Chase had also had plenty of bad times in that house, too. When he drank, his father could get mean. When he drank, his father had a temper.

When he got out of the truck and looked around, something hit Hunter's gut. There were crossroad moments in a person's life—this felt like one for him.

Inside the farmhouse, they sat at Linda's kitchen

table, a bit wobbly now as it was sitting on floor-boards that had sagged over time.

"What's the news?" Hunter asked his friend.

Chase popped the top off a bottle of beer and handed it to him. After he grabbed a beer for himself, his friend joined him at his mother's wobbly table. The table, like the kitchen, seemed so much smaller than he remembered. But then again, most of the time he had spent at this table, he had been a kid.

Chase held up his bottle of beer. "To Molly and Skyler."

Hunter touched his bottle to Chase's. "To Molly and Skyler."

Chase was the first person he had told about his relationship with Skyler. To his mind, Chase was the only one who wouldn't judge his feelings for her. After all, he had fallen for Molly in record time.

"Molly sent me some ideas for a ring," Chase said. "As soon as I sell this place, the first thing I'm doing is buying her the best damn ring I can afford."

Hunter took a swig of his beer then put the bottle down on the table. The table wobbled again.

"How can you stand not to fix this?" He stood up, grabbed one of the bottle caps on the counter, kneeled down and put the cap under one of the table's legs.

"This table is the least of my problems," Chase said.

Hunter jiggled the table to see how well the bottle cap had worked. Satisfied, he sat back down.

"What's the news on your end?" Chase asked him, milking his beer, as he had done for years now.

Hunter breathed in and let it on a frustrated sigh. "We're stuck, bro. That's the news. As long as her dad is laid up, she's not willing to even consider coming back here."

"Is she worth the wait to you?"

Hunter finished his beer. "Yeah, she's worth the wait. Problem is, I miss her."

They sat together in silence, each occupied with their own thoughts. Sometimes a person just needed a chance to see a problem from a different angle— that's what coming to the Rocking R had done for Hunter.

"I'm going to help you get the money for that ring right now," he told his friend.

Chase raised an eyebrow at him, his fingers busy peeling the wrapper off the bottle.

"I haven't spent a dime of my *Cowboy Up!* money."

His friend shook his head. "I'm not taking another dime from anybody. Not even you."

"I'm not talking about borrowing."

"Charity."

"Not charity. A business transaction."

"Come again?" Chase said, but Hunter knew he had his friend's full attention now.

"I'm going to buy the Rocking R."

Just now, sitting in the Rockwell kitchen, Hunter

finally knew what he wanted to do with all that money he had made from a show he had learned to regret. If he could buy the Rocking R Ranch, which would allow Chase to get that ring for Molly and help him establish his life in New York, then being on that damn show would actually have been worth it.

Chase stopped peeling the label and sat back in his chair. "You want to buy this place?"

"I do," he said. "I'll take the whole damn lot. What's your price?"

His friend did not respond the way Hunter had expected. He had expected Chase to be excited, relieved and, of course, to think that he had actually saved the day. Instead, Chase frowned and shook his head.

"Nope," he said.

"What do you mean *nope*?"

"Nope," Chase repeated. "I'm not going to let you buy this place just to bail me out. Forget it."

"I'm not buying it to bail you out."

Chase shot him a skeptical look.

"Okay, I admit that one of the results of buying this place would be to bail you out. But that's not the only reason."

His friend finished his beer and stood up. "Give me another reason."

"I'm years away from building on my stake at

Sugar Creek. I could move right into this place. I could move Skyler right into this place."

Chase put another beer down in front of him, grabbed his empty bottle and put it in the sink. His friend didn't get a second beer for himself.

"You want to live with Skyler here?"

"Yeah. Why not? I'll look a heck of a lot more tempting with an actual house instead of a trailer. Right?"

"I can't deny that." Chase laughed. "That trailer is not exactly a benefit to marrying you."

Hunter wasn't offended by his friend's friendly ribbing about his trailer; after all, it was true. He wanted to have a place for Skyler, a place where they could start their lives. They could save and design their perfect miniranch among the ancient oak trees while they occupied their time refurbishing the Rocking R.

"You really want to buy this place?" He could tell that his friend was starting to warm to the idea.

"Yeah," he said after he swallowed a swig of beer. "I can't let this place be sold to strangers. That way, it will stay in the family. And you'll always have a place to come home to when you bring Molly out to Montana for a visit."

"We can settle on a price that's fair," Chase said and that was when Hunter knew that his friend was on board with the idea.

Hunter held his hand out over the tabletop. "Do we have a deal?"

Chase shook his hand with the grip of a man who had done hard work all of his life. "We have a deal."

Hunter finished his second beer, stood up, tossed the bottle into the sink and then said, "Let's go take that damn sign out of the ground."

Chase stood up with a sigh, "Bro, I wish you had figured all of this out *before* I dug that hole."

"I like your hair," Hunter said to Skyler.

She reached up and touched her newly cut hair. "Do you? Molly's mom cut it for me."

"I like it short," he told her, wishing that he could reach through the screen and touch her.

"I kind of do, too," she agreed. "I always wore it long but now I think it suits me."

Once Hunter came up with a plan, he didn't want to wait to put it in action. While Skyler was busy getting her father set up with therapists, he had been busy buying the Rocking R Ranch. It had been a simple transaction—he was a cash buyer, not negotiating on the terms and he didn't give a damn about an inspection report. He knew the Rockwell home inside and out; he knew where all the bodies were buried in the plumbing, in the foundation and the roof.

"I have some news," he told her.

"Oh, yeah?" She settled back on her couch, which was her usual position when they talked.

"I bought the Rocking R Ranch."

Skyler's lavender-blue eyes widened. "You did?"

He nodded. "It's ours."

"Ours?" She repeated the word.

"It's a place to start."

Skyler had a confused look on her face. "Hunter—a place to start what?"

"Our lives together," he said directly.

"But we've talked about this," she said with a frown. "You know I can't even consider coming back to Montana until things are more stable around here. And even then…"

"Even then what?" Hunter asked, wondering why neither Chase nor Skyler had been as enthusiastic about his grand plan as he was.

She bit her lip, something she did when she was hesitating to say something to him.

"Even then what?" he repeated, prodding her to open up to him.

"I'm not going to move my whole entire life to Montana unless we were going to get married, Hunter." She held up her hand quickly. "And I'm not saying that to prompt some proposal out of you…"

"Is that all?" he asked, a light bulb coming on his brain. In his excitement, he had missed a vital step with Skyler.

"Is that all?" Now she was repeating the question. "It's kind of a big thing."

He leaned forward so she could see him more clearly in the video. "You want to marry me, don't you?"

When she didn't answer him right away, he came at it from a different angle. "I want to marry you."

"You do?"

"Of course I do. I thought you would have picked up on that by now."

"You have never mentioned marriage to me. Not once," Skyler told him.

"Well, let's fix that right now," Hunter said, and at that moment, Daisy jumped up on the small table in his trailer, walked in front of the camera and hit him in the face with her tail.

"Daisy!" Skyler exclaimed. "Hi, baby girl!"

Hunter gently moved the cat out of the way. "Will you marry me, Skyler?"

He couldn't read Skyler's expression—was she happy or mad?

Daisy had turned around and was rubbing up against his chin, purring and blocking the camera shot with her body.

"Damn it, Daisy. I'm trying to get something done here."

Hunter scooped up the cat and put her down on the floor with a quick pat he hoped would satisfy the feline for a moment or two.

"What do you think?" he asked, wondering why Skyler hadn't yet responded to his proposal.

"Well…" Skyler said slowly, thoughtfully. "I think this isn't the most romantic proposal on record. But yes, Hunter. I want to marry you."

A huge smile came to his face.

"But—"

"No buts."

"*But* we have to talk about my health, Hunter. Whenever I've tried to bring it up, you change the subject."

"You're in remission. Subject closed."

"Hunter—it's not that simple. I need to have regular checkups. I'm in remission, but there aren't any guarantees. If it…" She paused, swallowed her own worries back and then restarted. "If it comes back, can you handle it?"

"I can handle it, Skyler," Hunter said seriously. "In sickness and health. Remember?"

She smiled at him then. "Yes. In sickness and in health."

"So, is that a 'yes, I will marry you' smile?"

"Yes." Her smile widened. "I will marry you, Hunter."

"Hot damn." The cowboy grinned at her. "We're gonna get married, you and me."

"But we have to wait until after I get things settled with my dad, Hunter. You understand that I have no idea how long that will take."

"That's okay," he said. "You're worth the wait."

That brought a lovely smile to Skyler's lovely face. "Thank you, Hunter. You've always been worth the wait for me."

Chapter Sixteen

"Hey, Dad," Skyler said as she picked up the phone. "Everything okay?"

"Everything's fine," her father said with an annoyed sigh. Her hovering had increasingly annoyed Chester and she had really been working hard to hide her worry from him. "Come to the house when you have a moment."

"I'll be right there." Skyler had been taking care of the garage's bookkeeping from home and she was just at the point where she could take a break. Her father hadn't objected to her taking care of the books for now, but he had been diametrically opposed to her going back to work in the garage.

Skyler crossed quickly to the house, hurriedly

opened the back door and headed toward the living room, where her father spent most of his time. She rounded the corner and then stopped in her tracks.

"Hi, Skyler."

There he was—the cowboy of her dreams, standing in her living room. Wearing, as he always did, his boots, jeans and button-down shirt, tucked in. And his hat was on the couch next to where he had been sitting.

"We have a visitor," Chester said casually from his recliner.

Skyler put her hand over her mouth and swallowed back happy tears.

"Do you know how easy it is to get a COVID test around here?" he asked, walking toward her.

She nodded and met him halfway. They embraced, but he didn't kiss her, which was how she wanted it. They would kiss later, when they were alone.

After they hugged, he looked down into her face. "Surprised?"

"Floored," she admitted. "What are you doing here? How did you pull this off without me knowing?"

"He got in touch with me," Chester said, turning the TV on mute.

Together, Skyler sat down on the couch with Hunter, their hands intertwined, their shoulders and thighs touching. She couldn't stop looking at him; he was real.

"Your dad helped me keep it a secret," Hunter said. "Chase has come to propose to Molly."

"Oh." She welled up again. "I'm so happy for her."

Chester didn't seem surprised when Skyler suggested that she give Hunter a tour of her childhood home.

"Where are you staying?" she asked him.

"I have a hotel room with Chase. But I have a feeling he's going to be wanting some privacy."

"Yes." Skyler nodded.

"So your dad said I could stay in your old bedroom upstairs."

That made Skyler laugh. Of course, her old-fashioned father would agree to Hunter staying with them, as long as he wasn't staying with *her* in the apartment. No doubt Chester knew that they had been intimate, but he wasn't modern enough to condone it under his own roof.

She showed him the upstairs, including her very girly room, still decorated from high school, with small pink-rosebud wallpaper, antique lace curtains and a twin-size bed. Hunter sat down on her bed and looked around curiously at her room.

"I've never had a boy in this room before," she noted.

Hunter brought his eyes back to her with a possessive glint in his eye; she could tell he liked the fact that he was the first.

"I have to show you something," she said, "but you have to promise that you won't judge me and you won't let it influence, in any way, your decision to marry me."

The way he grinned at her let her know that his interest had been peaked. "What is it?"

Skyler opened her closet door, raised up on her tiptoes and pulled out a large photo album at the bottom of a stack of books on the shelf. She held the photo album tightly to her body, protectively, as she turned toward him.

"This might be a huge mistake."

"Well," he said. "Now you *have* to show me."

She walked over to him slowly and then held out the heavy album to him. She sat down next to him and leaned into his body as he opened up to the first page of the album. The only thing on the first page was a large signed promotional picture of him on the show *Cowboy Up!* with a large heart drawn around it in sparkling red ink. Hunter stared at that picture, a picture that he had signed so many years ago.

"I wrote to you for an autographed picture and you actually sent one to me," she told him, feeling a mixture of embarrassment and wonder that she was able to show him the picture now.

Still silent, Hunter turned the page and found the letter that he had sent along with the picture.

"I wrote this," he said, examining the letter more closely.

"You did?" she asked, unbelievingly. "I always figured your manager wrote it and you signed it."

"No." He shook his head. "This is my handwriting."

Hunter continued through the album that she had dedicated to the object of her affection: Hunter Brand from *Cowboy Up!* After they looked through all of the pictures and articles printed from the internet, Hunter closed the book, left it sitting on his lap and looked over at her with a strange expression on his face.

"I had a big crush on you," she said by way of explanation to fill in the awkward silence. "Well, not *you* really. The TV-show version of you."

Hunter appeared to be rendered speechless.

"Did I scare you?" She tugged her book out of his hands and carried it back to the closet. When she turned back around, he was standing up. In the small room, it was easy for him to reach for her and pull her into his arms. With a smirk on his face, he kissed her, long and deep.

"You don't scare me," he said, looking into her eyes. "Being without you scares me."

She wrapped her arms around him, so happy to be back in them. He took her face in his hands, wanting more of her kisses.

"Where is this apartment of yours?" he asked against her lips.

"Out back."

"We have to go there now." He buried his face in her neck. "Unless you want to finally christen this sweet little bed of yours."

The next night, Chester ordered takeout and invited Chase and Molly to join the three of them for dinner. Molly had a postengagement glow; Chase had given her the exact proposal she had always wanted—he got down on bended knee in Central Park. The conversation flowed easily and for the first time in a long time, the house was filled with laughter. Skyler could tell that Chester liked both of the men sitting at his table. Her father's approval of her future husband wasn't essential, but it was important.

"Pass me some of those potatoes," Chester said boisterously, noticeably uplifted by the company in his house.

Skyler didn't say a word. This night wasn't about trying to regulate her father's diet, a bone of contention between them—it was about celebrating Chase and Molly's engagement.

"So when are you two going to tie the knot?" her father asked Molly and Chase, using his right hand to scoop up potatoes instead of his left.

"Not for a while," Molly said as she and Chase

exchanged a smile. "I want a big wedding. Lots of planning."

"And I have to move out here and find a job," Chase added.

"What kind of work will you be looking for, son?" Chester asked before he took a big bite of potatoes loaded with gravy.

"I'm not sure. Whatever I can get to get myself established."

Hunter said, "Chase was a mechanic in the army."

Chester and Skyler turned their keen attention to Chase.

"What kind of training do you have?" her father asked.

Chase wiped his mouth off with a napkin before he answered. "Diesel mechanic. I worked on M1 Abrams tanks and every truck that the army owns. If it's a diesel I can fix it."

"Well…" Chester sat back in his chair and Skyler could tell that his wheels, like hers, were turning. "You didn't get marine training."

"No, sir." Chase smiled.

"But I imagine the army taught you how to at least hold a wrench right."

"Yes, sir. They did."

"I've got a job waiting for you if you want it." Her father rested his forearms on the table and looked Chase directly in the eye. "But I'll need you ASAP.

I'm laid up for a while and I need a solid diesel mechanic to pick up my slack."

Molly reached for Chase's hand. "I'd be honored to work for you, sir."

"Call me Sarge," Chester said.

After dinner, Skyler had shooed him out of the kitchen while she cleaned up, and Hunter took the opportunity to speak with Chester alone.

"I appreciate the hospitality," he told Skyler's father. Chester was a good man—stern but fair. And it was obvious that Skyler was the apple of Chester's eye.

"Well—" Chester turned the TV on mute "—I appreciate you taking such good care of Skyler while she was in Montana."

Hunter nodded, finding now that he was alone with Chester again that it was difficult to formulate the words he needed to say.

"I'd like to be able to take care of Skyler..." Hunter said quietly. "For the rest of her life."

Chester looked over at him, his eyes narrowed a bit, before he turned off the TV. "Speak your piece, son."

"I'd like your permission to marry Skyler."

Chester thought for a minute or two, time that seemed to stretch out much too long for Hunter's comfort.

"I'd like for Skyler to go to college. She left to help me take care of her mother. I've always regretted that for her," Chester said. "You got a problem with that?"

"No, sir."

"Are you planning on setting up house in Montana?"

"Yes, sir," Hunter said, not sure if Chester would be happy to hear this news or not. "I just bought a little place outside of Bozeman. A place that we can make our own."

"Good. Good." Chester nodded. "She was better in Montana. Happier. And, she couldn't—" Skyler's father waved his hand "—hover over me like she is now. I don't want her to waste her time trying to manage my life when she should be out living her own."

Chester pushed forward so the recliner was upright; he looked over at him. "I'm too damn old to have my daughter telling me to eat my vegetables."

Hunter laughed. "Yes, sir."

"Come with me." Chester stood up, a bit unsteady at first, but he found his balance quickly. Hunter followed the man to a bedroom down a hallway. Chester opened the top nightstand drawer, grabbed a box and then handed it to him.

"Give this to Skyler when the time is right."

Hunter opened the box and inside was a diamond ring. A round cut stone set in antique platinum.

"It was her mother's ring."

Hunter closed the box and tucked it into his pocket.

"Thank you, sir," Hunter said. "I love your daughter very much."

"Good." Chester nodded, turning his head but not soon enough. Hunter saw tears in the man's eyes. "Very good."

Chester cleared his throat several times before he brought his eyes back to his, "You understand that she's going to need doctors, specialists—we aren't completely out of the woods with this damn cancer business."

"I've already got doctors lined up for Skyler, sir. We can set up appointments for right after she arrives. Get her established."

Chester put his hand on his shoulder for a moment. "You'll take care of her."

"Yes, sir. I will."

"I'm counting on you," Skyler's father said. "Make her happy, keep her healthy."

They walked out to the living room and Chester stopped by the kitchen. "Come join us."

Skyler looked at Hunter curiously and wiped her hands on a nearby dishtowel. "Okay."

She sat next to Hunter on the couch while Chester eased back into his chair.

"I want you to go back to Montana with Hunter."

Skyler's eyes darted between her father and Hunter. Hunter looked legitimately shocked because he hadn't discussed a timeline with Chester.

"Dad—" Skyler began to protest.

"No." Chester cut her off. "You get your way with me all the time, Sky. This time it's my turn. I can't have you wringing your hands and micromanaging my appointments or counting my calories. You've always been so busy telling me how grown you are—well, in case you haven't noticed, I'm pretty damn well grown, too."

Skyler opened her mouth to say something, but Chester was determined to stay on center stage.

"Now, Hunter here is a nice young man. I like him. And even though he didn't have to, he's asked me for your hand in marriage and I've said yes."

The longer Chester talked, the younger Hunter felt. It was like the two of them were sitting in the principal's office after they'd got caught making out in the bleachers.

"Hunter tells me he bought a nice little place for the two of you. So go on and get on with it."

"Dad…" Skyler began again.

Chester looked lovingly at his daughter; this look tempered the gruffness of his words. "I love you, Sky. You were happy in Montana—when you're happy, I'm happy. If you want to do something to help me get better, go back to Montana. Go be happy."

Wordlessly, Skyler stood up and hugged her father. "I love you, Dad."

It was a long, poignant hug, a hug between two

people who had leaned on each other to navigate some of their darkest days.

"Okay." Chester patted her on the back. "Now you two go on and try to stay out of trouble. My show is on."

"Molly, you aren't going to believe how perfect this house is for me." Skyler was video-chatting with her friend from the Rocking R Ranch.

"We can't believe that we got to move into your apartment!" Molly laughed joyfully. "We swapped."

"We did swap!" Skyler laughed, happy to be back in Montana with Hunter. "You've requested time off for the wedding, right? You have the dates?"

"Already taken care of. We will be there," her friend said. "I love you, Sky. I'll see you in a couple of months."

Skyler hung up the phone and looked around her new—*old*—farmhouse. This was to be her first home as a married woman and she couldn't feel luckier. With a lot of love, time and sweat equity, Hunter and she intended to restore the farmhouse to its original glory. Skyler finished washing the breakfast dishes and looked out the kitchen window to see Zodiac and Dream Catcher grazing in the pasture. Hunter had moved the horses to the property soon after they landed in Bozeman.

In the distance, she saw her husband-to-be walking toward the house carrying some tools he had used to repair one of the pasture fences. Eager to share the news from back home with Hunter, she grabbed her hat and raced out the front door. On the front porch, Daisy was sunning herself happily. The cat executed a barrel roll and then stretched out her legs and her toes. With a laugh, Skyler rubbed the cat's belly, so happy to have her feline friend living with them at the Rocking R. She skipped down the steps and met Hunter in the yard.

They greeted with a kiss and a hug, which was their way.

"I just heard from Molly." She fell in beside him as he walked toward a nearby barn that he had turned into his work shed.

"How's everything on their end?"

"They love the apartment. How awesome is it that we actually got to just swap houses?"

"Pretty awesome." He smiled at her.

"Chase is doing an incredible job for Dad, so he doesn't have to furlough any workers. And Dad is getting rent from Molly and Chase so…"

Hunter put his tools in his toolbox. "All is well that ends well?"

She wrapped her arms around him, not caring that he was dirty and sweaty. "Exactly."

Arm and arm, they walked together across the yard. She asked him, "What's on your agenda for today?"

"I actually want to head over to Sugar Creek.

Go pick some stuff up from the trailer. Did you get your application for Montana State done?" He held open the front door for her, the screen door creaking loudly. "I need to fix this," he said, fiddling with the latch.

"You've got to fix a ton of stuff," she agreed.

"So," he said, taking his hat off and hanging it on the hat rack. "Are you done with your application?"

"I was just about to hit Send when Molly called."

"Why don't you finish it while I take a shower? Then we'll head to Sugar Creek."

Her application to college completed, Skyler walked out to the pasture to visit with Zodiac and Dream Catcher. Jessie, Hunter's sister, had given Dream Catcher to her as a prewedding gift.

"Hi, sweet girl." The mare walked over to the fence where she was standing. She rubbed the horse between the eyes and then fed her a molasses treat out of her pocket.

"We are going to be together for the rest of your life," Skyler said to the mare, still in awe of the way her life had unfolded.

Soon Zodiac meandered up to the fence, poking his soft nose into her hand looking for a treat. She laughed, happy that Zodiac was still her miracle horse. According to Liam, he had made a miraculous full recovery and was cleared for easy trail rides. Hunter promised that they would go on their first trail ride as soon as he finished fixing the fence.

"There you are." Hunter found her watching the horses as they walked out to the middle of the pasture.

He put his arm around her and they stood together, in silence, gazing out at their new home. Skyler leaned her head over and rested it on his shoulder. "I feel happy here."

"I'm glad," he said, tightening his hold on her. "You ready to take a ride over to Sugar Creek with me?"

She nodded with a smile, knowing that this beautiful view was hers to enjoy for the rest of her days. They walked together to his truck, arm in arm, discussing, as they liked to do, their plans for the Rocking R. Inside the truck now, in her spot, Skyler buckled her seat belt.

"I think we need to start painting the inside of the house next week," she said when he joined her in the truck.

"We'll see." He cranked the engine. "Let me get things straightened around outside first."

"I'll help you straighten things around outside and then we can paint together next week."

He smiled at her as they left Rocking R land and pulled onto the highway that would lead them a short distance to Sugar Creek. "Sounds like a plan."

"Our gravel is holding," she said excitedly when they reached the main Sugar Creek Ranch road.

"You did a good job."

"Yes, I did!"

Hunter took the roughly hewn road that would lead them to his trailer. Skyler hadn't yet been back to the ancient Oak Tree Hill, where they had had their first amazing date. This was the place, she believed, that she truly fell in love with the real Hunter Brand.

Hand in hand, they walked beneath the canopy of the oak trees, and Skyler reveled in the cool breeze and sweet-smelling air that met them as they walked deeper into the embrace of the old trees.

"I love it here," she whispered, always feeling a reverence for this unique spot in the world.

"I love you." Hunter let her hand drop and he stopped walking. "And I really wish I could have given you a more romantic proposal."

"That's okay." Skyler turned around and discovered her cowboy kneeling before her.

"Skyler." Hunter held up a closed box. "Will you marry me?"

Her eyes immediately filled with tears as she nodded her head, too emotional to even get the word *yes* out of her mouth. Hunter flipped open the box and that was when she saw her mother's engagement ring inside.

Tears of joy and sorrow for her lost mother flowed

freely down her cheeks as Hunter stood and slid the ring onto her finger.

"Your father told me to give this to you when the time was right."

Still crying, Skyler gazed at the ring on her finger—a ring that symbolized a happy marriage between her mother and father. The ring also symbolized her father's approval of the man with whom she intended to spend the rest of her life.

Hunter wrapped his arms around her, hugged her tightly and then kissed her gently on the lips.

"Thank you for my proposal do-over, Hunter," she said between kisses.

"Anything for you, my love." Her dream cowboy said, "Anything for you."

Epilogue

Theirs was a simple ceremony beneath the canopy of the ancient oak trees where they had first fallen in love. Dr. Bonita DeLaFuente-Brand, Gabe's wife, arranged for her father's private jet to bring Molly, Chase and Chester to Bozeman, Montana, for an early fall wedding. The air was crisp and Skyler, to Hunter's mind, was the most beautiful bride Montana had ever seen. Her simple, unembellished white satin gown, complete with pockets, emphasized her narrow waist and complemented her short reddish-gold locks. His mother had handcrafted a pair of white leather moccasins, at Skyler's request, for the wedding. It was a gesture that had touched Lilly's heart, as it had touched his own.

Together, they stood hand in hand beneath the oldest of the ancient trees on his hill, with his family standing in a circle around them while the pastor had them read their vows. While Skyler was reading her vows to him, all Hunter could do was focus in on the softness of her lips, the pertness of her small nose, the little freckle on her left cheek and the darkness of her long lashes surrounding her unusual lavender-blue-gray eyes. She was the true love of his life—his first, only and forever.

"I now pronounce you husband and wife," the pastor said. "Hunter. You may now kiss your bride."

She smiled at him, her smile so warm and full of promise of the good years to come. He leaned down and pressed his lips to hers. It was a sweet kiss, tender and kind.

"I love you," Skyler said, holding his gaze.

"I love you," he said, stealing one more kiss before they faced, for the first time, their friends and family as husband and wife.

The Rocking R Ranch was right now, but one day, they would build their dream home right here on this hill. One day, their children would race across those fields, carefree and completely loved. One day, Hunter would meet his grandchildren—a new generation of Brands with his determination and Skyler's kindness.

They had decided on a picnic-style reception at the main house. Next to Skyler, Hunter sat at a table for two at the top of a horseshoe shape of tables.

"What did you get Skyler for a wedding present?" Savannah called out to him.

"I got her what she asked for," he said, and Skyler was beaming as she thought of her wedding present. "I got her a skid steer."

"It was the best present of my life!" she called out to her friends and family. As their wedding party laughed, Skyler turned her pretty violet eyes to him.

"This feels like a dream," his bride said with a happy sigh.

He took her lovely face in his hands, her eyes so full of love for him. Hunter said, "My beloved Skyler. You are my every dream come true."

* * * * *

*For more sweeping Western romances,
try these great stories:*

His Forever Texas Rose
by Stella Bagwell

Making Room for the Rancher
by Christy Jeffries

Their Night to Remember
by Judy Duarte

*Available now wherever
Harlequin Special Edition books
and ebooks are sold.*

WE HOPE YOU ENJOYED
THIS BOOK FROM

HARLEQUIN
SPECIAL
EDITION

Believe in love. Overcome obstacles. Find happiness.

Relate to finding comfort and strength in the
support of loved ones and enjoy the journey
no matter what life throws your way.

6 NEW BOOKS AVAILABLE EVERY MONTH!

COMING NEXT MONTH FROM

⬧ HARLEQUIN
SPECIAL EDITION

Available March 30, 2021

#2827 RUNAWAY GROOM
The Fortunes of Texas: The Hotel Fortune • by Lynne Marshall
When Mark Mendoza discovers his fiancée cheating on him on their wedding day, he hightails it out of town. Megan Fortune is there to pick up the pieces—and to act as his faux girlfriend when his ex shows up. Mark swears he will never get involved again. Megan doesn't want to be a "rebound" fling. But they find each other irresistible. What's a fake couple to do?

#2828 A NEW FOUNDATION
Bainbridge House • by Rochelle Alers
While restoring a hotel with his adoptive siblings, engineer Taylor Williamson hires architectural historian Sonja Rios-Martin. Neither of them ever thought they'd mix business with pleasure, but when their passion runs into both of their pasts, they'll have to figure out if this passion is worth fighting for.

#2829 WYOMING MATCHMAKER
Dawson Family Ranch • by Melissa Senate
Divorced real estate agent Danica Dunbar still isn't ready for marriage and motherhood. When she has to care for her infant niece, Ford Dawson, the sexy detective who wants to settle down, is a little too helpful. Will this matchmaker pawn him off on someone else? Or is she about to make a match of her own?

#2830 THE RANCHER'S PROMISE
Match Made in Haven • by Brenda Harlen
Mitchell Gilmore was best man at Lindsay Delgado's wedding, "uncle" to her children and, when Lindsay is tragically widowed, a consoling shoulder. Until one electric kiss changes everything. Now Mitchell is determined to move from lifelong friendship to forever family. It's a risky proposition, but maybe Lindsay will finally make good on her promise.

#2831 THE TROUBLE WITH PICKET FENCES
Lovestruck, Vermont • by Teri Wilson
A pregnant former beauty queen and a veteran fire captain at the end of his rope realize it's never too late to build a family and that life, love and lemonade are sweeter when you let down your guard and open your heart to fate's most unexpected twists and turns.

#2832 THEIR SECOND-CHANCE BABY
The Parent Portal • by Tara Taylor Quinn
Annie Morgan needs her ex-husband's help—specifically, she needs him to sign over his rights to the embryos they had frozen prior to their divorce. But when she ends up pregnant—with twins—it becomes very clear their old feelings never left. Will their previous problems wreck their relationship once again?

YOU CAN FIND MORE INFORMATION ON UPCOMING HARLEQUIN TITLES, FREE EXCERPTS AND MORE AT HARLEQUIN.COM.

HSECNM0321

Mitchell Gilmore and Lindsay Delgado had been best friends for as long as they could remember. He was best man at her wedding, "uncle" to her children and, when Lindsay is tragically widowed, a consoling shoulder. Until one electric kiss changes everything. Now Mitchell is determined to move from lifelong friendship to forever family—if Lindsay can see that he's ready to be a family man...

Read on for a sneak peek at
The Rancher's Promise
by Brenda Harlen,
the new book in her Match Made in Haven series!

"Do you want coffee?" Lindsay asked.

"No, thanks."

"So...how was your date?"

Considering that it was over before nine o'clock, she was surprised when Mitchell said, "Actually, it was great. It turns out that Karli's not just beautiful but smart and witty and fun. We had a great dinner and interesting conversation."

She didn't particularly want to hear all the details, but she'd been the one to insist they remain firmly within the friend zone and, as a friend, it was her duty to listen.

"That is great," she said. Lied. "I'm happy for you." Another lie. "But I have to wonder, if she's so great… why are you here?"

"Because she's not you," he said simply. "And I don't want anyone but you."

She might have resisted the words, but the intensity and sincerity of his gaze sent them arrowing straight to her heart. Still, she had to be smart. To think about what was at stake.

"I know you're afraid to risk our friendship, and I understand why. But there's so much more we could have together. So much more we could be to one another. Don't we deserve a chance to find out?"

Before Lindsay could respond to either his confession or his question, he was kissing her.

Don't miss
The Rancher's Promise *by Brenda Harlen,*
available April 2021 wherever
Harlequin Special Edition books and ebooks are sold.

Harlequin.com

HSEEXP0321

Love Harlequin romance?

DISCOVER.

Be the first to find out about promotions, news and exclusive content!

Facebook.com/HarlequinBooks

Twitter.com/HarlequinBooks

Instagram.com/HarlequinBooks

Pinterest.com/HarlequinBooks

ReaderService.com

EXPLORE.

Sign up for the Harlequin e-newsletter and download a free book from any series at **TryHarlequin.com**

CONNECT.

Join our Harlequin community to share your thoughts and connect with other romance readers! **Facebook.com/groups/HarlequinConnection**

HSOCIAL2020